THE BLACKM

ISABEL COLEGATE was born in 1931 in London and was educated at Runton Hill School in Norfolk. In 1952 she went into partnership with Anthony Blond, who was then starting a literary agency and would go on to found a publishing house, and in 1953 she married her husband Michael Briggs, with whom she has a daughter and two sons.

Colegate's first novel, *The Blackmailer*, was published by Blond in 1958 and was followed by two more novels focusing on English life in the years after the Second World War: *A Man of Power* (1960) and *The Great Occasion* (1962). These were later republished by Penguin in an omnibus volume, *Three Novels*, in 1983.

Though she has written a number of other successful novels, as well as reviews for the *Spectator*, *Daily Telegraph* and *Times Literary Supplement*, Colegate is best known for her bestseller and major critical success *The Shooting Party* (1980), which won the W. H. Smith Literary Award and was adapted for a now-classic 1985 film version. The book is still in print today (with Counterpoint in the US and as a Penguin Modern Classic in the UK). More recently, she has written the acclaimed novel *Winter Journey* (1995) and the nonfiction work *Pelican in the Wilderness: Hermits and Solitaries* (2002).

Isabel Colegate was elected a Fellow of the Royal Society of Literature in 1981. She and her husband live in Somerset.

By Isabel Colegate

The Blackmailer (1958)

A Man of Power (1960)

The Great Occasion (1962)

Statues in a Garden (1964)

Orlando King (1968)

Orlando at the Brazen Threshold (1971)

Agatha (1973)

News from the City of the Sun (1979)

The Shooting Party (1980)

A Glimpse of Sion's Glory (1985)

Deceits of Time (1988)

The Summer of the Royal Visit (1991)

Winter Journey (1995)

A Pelican in the Wilderness (2002)

ISABEL COLEGATE

THE BLACKMAILER

WITH A NEW FOREWORD BY THE AUTHOR

VALANCOURT BOOKS

The Blackmailer by Isabel Colegate
First published London: Anthony Blond, 1958
First Valancourt Books edition 2014

Published by Valancourt Books, Richmond, Virginia
http://www.valancourtbooks.com

All Valancourt Books publications are printed on acid-free paper
that meets all ANSI standards for archival quality paper.

ISBN 978-1-941147-22-1 (*trade paperback*)
Also available as an electronic book.

Set in Dante MT 10.5/12.5
Cover by M. S. Corley

FOREWORD

The Blackmailer was first published in 1958. Anthony Blond had just started his own publishing firm. I think *The Blackmailer* was in his second swathe, the first having consisted of Simon Raven's *The Feathers of Death*, Burgo Partridge's *History of Orgies* and I think Gillian Freeman's *The Liberty Man*. Anthony had previously been a literary agent, in which capacity I was his partner, on the strength of having contributed £50 towards the initial expenses. We had an office in New Bond Street, at the top of a small building behind Barclays Bank. On the floor below was the office of Goya Perfumes, whose products sometimes suffused the air with floral essences, competing with the smell of burnt milk which came from the room beyond ours, where Major Clare, the theatrical agent, liked hot milk with his coffee. On the other side of the passage was a solicitor whose son, the actor David Tomlinson, would occasionally bound energetically up the stairs quite as if he were still playing a part in *Chitty Chitty Bang Bang*. Major Clare and his partner Mr. Fitch had to walk through our room to reach their own, and most considerately would do so on tiptoe so as not to disturb my Cavalier King Charles spaniel, asleep in front of the gas fire. The dog in *The Blackmailer* is a real dog, but the other characters are not real people. Fiction is not at all the same story as biography and there has to be room for invention as well as for manipulation in the service of a theme. I suppose most characters in novels are likely to be composites of people one has known or met, people one has read about or glimpsed on a bus, and oneself. Sometimes readers find this hard to believe. Certainly the editor at Jonathan Cape who rejected *The Blackmailer* before Anthony published it was convinced that I must have known André Deutsch, a well-known contemporary publisher whom I never met. Jonathan Cape himself seemed keen to publish the book, though he warned me that no one could expect to earn any money from a first novel, and that though some people said things might look up at the third, he himself thought one usually had to wait until the fifth. I was quite happy at this prospect, but unfortunately at a subsequent interview his chief editor Robert Knittel told me that Jonathan Cape was on the point of retirement and that he himself believed that there was no good fiction to be found in England and that America was the only hope. He said that I could console myself by the thought that he had rejected Françoise Sagan's *Bonjour Tristesse*, a current best seller. I was not at all consoled, but other things intervened. In 1956 my daughter was born and in 1958 Anthony, having briefly worked for Allen Wingate while we wound down the agency, began his own imprint.

Looking back at the book fifty-seven years later I can see that the character of Feliks Hanescu must in fact have emerged from something in the air in our upstairs room. I was incapacitated by shyness in those days and seldom emerged into the outside world except to take the dog for a walk in Green Park. Otherwise I dealt with the correspondence in the office, assumed a fearsomely cool and repressive voice on the telephone which I felt implied a large staff behind me, and read and reported on the manuscripts which were sent to us. The reports must have been depressing for the writers to read because my standards were impossibly high. Anthony meanwhile would venture out into the cut and thrust of the literary world, returning with the tales which I suppose provided the material for the character of Feliks. That world has changed, become more professional, more fiercely commercial and more conventional. Feliks of course is a creature of fantasy but characters not immeasurably different could adorn the publishing trade in those days. After all Robert Knittel believed Feliks Hanescu to be a portrait of André Deutsch.

At the time I was writing the book the French troubles in Indo-China had been in the news. The battle of Dien Bien Phu, which put an end to French influence in Vietnam, featured at some point a siege and a gallant officer. Was there some kind of rumour about that gallant officer? Perhaps that started me thinking about different forms of betrayal and then perhaps the soup of the stuff of dreams began to bubble. It bubbles less easily now that I am old, which is why I look back on *The Black-mailer* with a certain affection.

Isabel Colegate
February 24, 2014

I

'Brilliant performance,' said the brown man, expansively. 'Masterly, I'd have said. Never thought you'd do it, quite frankly. You must meet all my errant acquaintances.'

'No, I'm sorry. I meant to do better for you,' said Baldwin Reeves, who looked indeed disgruntled and rather puffy in the face. 'I thought I'd get you off altogether; but Fortescue's always hard on motoring offences. We'd have been all right with Lamb.'

'Nonsense, my dear fellow, I'm delighted,' said the other. 'What's a tenner between enemies? I really thought I'd lose my licence this time.'

They paused at the bottom of the steps of Bow Street Magistrates Court. Mr. Parker was just back from a skiing holiday, was off again to the south of France to lose his manly tan in the casinos while the spring crept north. Baldwin had had a hard cold winter, and it showed in his face and his frame of mind. Parker had hit an old woman on a pedestrian crossing on his way home one evening in his new Ford Thunderbird from some boisterous outing with the boys. The old woman had luckily lived, but Parker had a nasty driving record, so Baldwin's case had not been easy. Baldwin disliked, despised and envied his client, but would have liked to have got him an absolute discharge because he was the sort of person whose partisanship was not to be sneezed at.

'I must be getting along,' said Parker. 'Lunching with some old fiend of an ambassadress—ah well, big lunch . . . I really can't thank you enough, really most grateful. See you in the club some time.'

Baldwin thought, rich people are always mean. Outwardly affable, he watched the brown man stride springily away from him towards his car. 'You'd have thought he'd have given me lunch,' he thought, 'and anyway I know ambassadresses too.'

He took a taxi to Fleet Street, meaning to walk down to his chambers in Paper Buildings. It was a cold, bleak, hopeless sort of day, and he had a case coming up that afternoon which he knew he was bound to lose. The taxi put him down in Fleet Street: on his way towards the Inner Temple he went into a pub and asked for a sandwich and a glass of beer.

The place was full of newspaper men and lawyers of one sort or another. Baldwin sat down at a table next to a group of students engaged on just recognisable imitations of a well-known law tutor.

He disliked eating alone. It was partly a question of appearances: he would rather people saw him with someone else, because it gave a better impression and made him seem busy and sought-after; but there was more to it than that. Eating alone reminded him of the bleak years of the beginning of his struggle, of the baked beans consumed in Lyons Tea Shops in those unrelievedly awful days when no one had heard of him, when he looked round at the old women, the shop-girls and the workmen, the intellectuals, the lunatics, the lovers, and thought, with a depth of conflicting emotion which brought tears to his eyes, 'I'll show you, you wait, I'll just show you,' and at the same time, 'I'll help you, I'll look after you, leave it to me,' and 'You'll acknowledge me, everyone of you, not a life but will be touched by mine,' and at the same time, 'I will get you out of this, I will give you hope.'

But his own hopes were perhaps not quite what they had been. The struggle was turning out harder than he had anticipated, or if not harder (for he had been prepared for anything) then longer; and there was a bitterness and a doubt of misdirection which he had not used to have. There seemed to be a lack of response, an indifference, at the heart of things, which gave his earlier ambitions, ruthless though he had meant them to be, the aspect of ideals.

Of course this was a bad day, a sour unprofitable day, to be got through and forgotten as quickly as possible. At least he could have a very small lunch, and that might count as an achievement, since he was greedy though anxious not to be fat.

Finishing his sandwich, he took an exercise book out of his dispatch case and looked at the notes he had scribbled that morning for his big speech the next day. He was nursing a 'marginal' constituency, and reading through his notes his spirits suddenly rose—they were not so bad after all, the agent was sure there would be a big attendance for once, and that television fellow was going to be there so as to have a word with him afterwards; he could do with a television appearance just at the moment.

In this more hopeful frame of mind he greeted with a polite smile the girl who, disengaging herself from the group of now departing students, accosted him with a nervous smile and said: 'Aren't you Baldwin Reeves?'

'You want my autograph I suppose?' said Baldwin, appreciating with his mind's eye the charmingly quizzical lift of his eyebrows.

'Oh well,' the girl said, embarrassed. 'Really, I wanted to ask you about—that is, Lucy Fuller said she knew you—d'you know her?'

'Of course, dear Lucy,' said Baldwin. 'How is she?'

'Oh terribly well,' said the girl, her nervous soft glance sliding away from him. 'She's having a baby. Did you—did you know Anthony Lane?'

'Yes,' said Baldwin, less affably.

'Oh,' she blushed. 'Yes, she said you did. I only met him once, just before he went abroad. I thought he was wonderful. It must have been wonderful to have known him properly, I mean like you did.' She spoke in a rushing series of gentle gasps.

'I see it's not me you admire after all,' said Baldwin sadly. Seeing she still awkwardly stood there, he added: 'Won't you sit down?'

'Oh well really I must go,' she said, sitting down.

'Have a drink?' said Baldwin. She was quite pretty, but her approach annoyed him—its immodesty was too coy. He put her down as a creature of no account: so, for that matter, was Lucy Fuller.

'No thank you,' she said. 'I suppose you don't like talking about it.'

'About drink?' said Baldwin. 'I don't mind.'

'No, Korea,' said the girl. 'I mean, it must have been so awful.'

'Oh yes,' said Baldwin, indifferently. 'Awful.' He began to draw a very bad likeness of her in the margin of his notes.

She looked hurt. 'I suppose you get tired of people gushing about him,' she said humbly. 'Only after all there are so few heroes these days and he is the one person everyone agrees was wonderful. I mean, isn't he?'

'He was a proper hero,' said Baldwin, still drawing. 'A proper hero.'

'You were with him all the time, I suppose—out there, I mean?' she said, her voice a little hushed.

'Not all the time,' said Baldwin, in the same sort of tone. 'There were times when he was where none of us could reach him—times when though we were there he was alone.'

'I see what you mean,' she breathed.

'My poor child,' said Baldwin, putting down his pencil and leaning back in his chair. 'Keep your hero—do you kiss his photograph every night?—but leave me out of it. I am a bad man.'

He suddenly leered at her, an awful base lecherous leer, and leaning towards her with a sort of buzzing sound, pinched her on the thigh. Then he burst into a great shout of laughter.

She stood up, blushing again and quite at a loss. 'Well, I'll—I'll tell Lucy I've seen you,' she said, beginning to edge away.

He waved foolishly, and she hurried out of the pub after her vanished friends. He went on laughing, his horrid gesture having given him a sense of huge release.

'Life's a splendid business,' he said to the small journalist who, passing on his way to the bar, had stopped to stare. 'A splendid business.'

'Come into money?' said the journalist, turning away to ask for a glass of beer.

'No,' said Baldwin.

The journalist came back with his beer. Baldwin knew

him quite well in a casual sort of way without being able to remember whether his surname was Harman or his Christian name Herman.

'As a matter of fact I've merely been very rude to a wholly inoffensive girl,' said Baldwin. 'It was unkind, but she unwittingly caught me on the raw, as the saying is. I'm a most resentful person, I'm afraid. I bear malice. Do you? Probably not, I should think.'

'Can't afford to in my job,' said Harman, (for it was, in fact, his surname). 'Got to have a rhinoceros hide. How's business? Anything juicy?'

'Nothing much for you I'm afraid,' said Baldwin.

'Nobody's nice confession?' Harman asked. 'A good, hot serial—that's what I want. You know we pay the top.'

'I don't believe you do,' said Baldwin. 'They paid me practically nothing for the only article I ever did for your paper, and then they mutilated it beyond recognition.'

'You must be full of society scandal, the way you get around,' said Harman.

'I only know one scandal, and that's an old one,' said Baldwin.

'How old?' asked Harman.

'Oh, years,' said Baldwin. 'It involves quite a lot of important names, though mainly military ones; it involves one hero and/or one traitor, and could be made to imply that the war in Korea was grossly mismanaged, and that all sorts of people were incompetent. I could make it quite dramatic, spin it out to quite a good length, and apart from anything else I'd be paying off an old score, an old sore score.'

'Write it,' said Harman. 'Write it, for God's sake.'

'Will your paper print it?' said Baldwin.

'How can I say if you don't tell me any more?' said Harman. 'Give me one name, one name involved.'

'Anthony Lane,' said Baldwin.

Harman looked surprised, then nodded.

'Sounds excellent,' he said. 'Excellent. Anthony Lane, eh? You know your facts, I suppose? You were there, of course. . . .'

'How much would they pay for that sort of thing?' asked Baldwin.

'A lot, if it's good,' said Harman. 'Look, write a synopsis, get a bit of authentication—you know the laws of libel better than I do—give me a ring and I'll arrange for you to see Blow, the Features Editor—nothing easier. Now do that, for God's sake. I like the sound of it very much, very much indeed. Anthony Lane, yes. He really was made into a hero, no one's forgotten him—and all that upper-class, smart regiment stuff—yes, I like the sound of some low-down on that very much indeed, just the stuff for us. We'll discuss how I come into it later, eh? I know you're on the level.' He finished his beer and stood up. 'Got to go,' he said. 'Write it. I'll see you get top rates, big money, really big, you take my word.'

When he had gone, Baldwin picked up the pencil which was still lying on the table in front of him, and turning over the page on which he had written the outline of his speech and drawn so unflatteringly Anthony Lane's admirer, he began casually to scribble some other notes. Even as he wrote he was not sure who, if anyone, would ever read what he was writing.

2

He was a little taken aback when the door was opened by a half-sized man wearing a beret and a mackintosh: it hardly seemed in keeping with the conventional exterior of the house, the clean olive-green door with its glittering brass-work, the rather self-conscious terracotta window-boxes full of frost-bitten primroses.

'Madame is upstairs. If you wait in here I will tell her.' So he was foreign as well as a midget, and perhaps it was one or other of those facts which had embittered him, for the look which he gave to the visitor before stumping out of the room was certainly venomous.

Baldwin looked about him, speculating. This French deformity—was he a servant, or what? He found it hard to imagine anyone wilfully choosing such an unattractive employee. It seemed therefore more likely—and the thinker hardly noticed the paradox—that he should be her lover. Besides, if he were a servant, surely he would be better dressed? The too-large navy-blue beret, the shabby brown belted mackintosh, floppy trousers and short thick shoes seemed by their audacious nastiness to indicate someone who was quite at home. Unless of course he was not a resident there at all, but someone called in to mend the electric light or clean the windows, and whose curious aspect would probably lose him her custom. He hoped so, because a lover, however small, would not suit his purpose; and indeed it seemed the most likely explanation, for the room in which he waited showed no sign of being lived in by an eccentric—nor even, on second thoughts, by a woman, for it was an austere greyish-brownish room with few pictures, many books, and an untidy desk in one corner. It was not, he was pleased to see, a shabby room: there were no outward signs of poverty. The white paintwork was too clean to have been done long ago, London dirt being what it is, and the furniture, though there was not much of it, was good. On the other hand there was no luxury: there were no flowers, for instance, and the cigarette boxes were empty. There were no shiny magazines, no gramophone or television set, and the Persian rugs on the floor, though good enough, might easily have come from one or other of the parents—the Lanes probably, since he had heard that hers were nothing to speak of—and he noticed, using a simple means test he had often found valid, that there was no fitted carpet.

He was still padding up and down the room when the midget reappeared and said: 'She comes directly. You sit down.' It was a villainous accent, probably not French after all, he thought, and was accompanied by a commanding gesture towards a chair.

'Thank you,' Baldwin said without moving.

The midget waited blankly, and they faced each other, fat man and dwarf, in deep dislike. A rustle of movement which raised Baldwin's hopes, making him think she must be light and airy, frilly and thin as he liked them, broke the silence, but it was only a dog, a dog who was light, airy, frilly, but not thin, and who wriggled up to Baldwin as if they were each other's greatest friends.

'Bertie!' said the midget as if it were some foul imprecation. The dog danced on. The midget in evident rage seized it by the collar and began to drag it from the room, the dog protesting with unexpectedly ferocious growls.

'Come out you Bertie,' the midget was saying. 'Sit down. Come on. Shut up.'

'It's all right, Jean-Claude,' a voice said in the hall. 'Bertie can come with me.'

Jean-Claude muttered something and a girl came into the room, Bertie behind her.

Baldwin was unreasonably disappointed: for what did it matter, after all, what she looked like? All the same it would have been more amusing if she had been attractive; but he realised at once that she was not his type. He had expected someone at least rather more distinguished. This might have been any little Chelsea girl passed on the way here—flat chest, straight hair, jeans and a sweater, nice eyes, but face too broad, big hands and feet—it was obvious that their relationship could only be a business one.

'So you are Judith,' he said expansively. 'About whom I have heard so much.'

'Oh have you?' she said indifferently. 'You telephoned didn't you?'

'I did, and you were out, and as I was passing on my way back from the week-end I thought I would look in on the chance of seeing you instead of waiting till tomorrow. You don't mind, I hope?'

'Of course not. Have a drink?' She opened a cupboard, and waving at it said: 'Perhaps you'd help yourself. Is it very cold in here? The fire's been going all day but it's still not warm enough, is it? Was it cold in the country?'

'Freezing,' he said. 'I was staying with the Millers—Gavin Miller—d'you know him?'

'No,' she said, without saying that she had heard of him, though obviously she had, because everyone had.

'They have a new central heating system which they're very boring about and which as far as I can see might as well not exist.'

The way in which she was hunched in her chair, one hand holding the dog very close to her legs, made him think she might already be uneasy. The thought crossed his mind that she might even know what he knew—but there was no one who could, or would, have told her, and if she did know she must have guessed. Besides that made no difference, his weapon would be no less powerful.

'Can't I pour out a drink for you?' he asked, thinking, hm, nothing but South African sherry. She refused, but accepted one of his cigarettes, and leaning back in her chair, stared at him for some moments before finally smiling and saying with a small sigh which might have been of resignation: 'So you were with Anthony.'

'I was with Anthony,' he sat opposite her. 'Of course the first thing I must do is tell you how desperately sorry I was that he died, not only because of my own affection for him, but because I knew he had not been married long.'

'Yes, it was very sad,' she said, with detachment, looking down.

'Of course we were all very fond of him,' said Baldwin.

'So many people were,' she said gently, as if anything he might have thought about her late husband was a matter of in-difference to her. This was not quite what he had expected, but after all there was a sort of familiarity about it: with Anthony too one's opinions had not mattered because he had been so sure of his own.

'I was his second-in-command, you see,' Baldwin went on.

He understood why she looked surprised, because although he had been only four years older than Anthony Lane he looked more and had besides a certain air of authority.

After a pause she seemed to feel that something more was

required of her, and, pulling the dog awkwardly on to her knee, she said: 'I had one letter from there, from where the fighting was I mean. I don't know whether he wrote more—I imagine he was pretty busy.'

'Yes, he was busy,' he said.

The look she gave him amazed him. 'She knows,' he thought. He was aware of two other things, that something in his voice had committed him more than he had meant it to, and that she was, quite simply, in his power. He was so excited that he trembled.

When he had savoured the moment for as long as he felt it wise, he stood up.

'Well, I really only came to introduce myself,' he said, his hands behind his back in front of the fireplace. 'The truth is, this is really more in the nature of a business call than anything else. I'm afraid I was presuming on my friendship with your husband to appeal to your good offices as one of the most successful publishers in London.'

'Oh, you've written a book?' she asked, with the lack of interest he was beginning to expect from her.

'Not a book so much as a newspaper story,' he said. 'Or at least that's how it is at the moment, and that's how I've presented it to my old friend Blow of the *Sunday News*. But he seemed so excited about it—more so than I'd expected—that it occurred to me that I might very well write it up into quite a startling book; and that's what I thought might interest you.'

'Of course, if it's startling,' she said. 'You've sold it to the *News* then?'

'Well, I've been going into the whole thing,' said Baldwin. 'And one or two people have told me that to sell the serial rights of a book before selling the book itself to a publisher is all wrong—the book loses half its value, and the publisher's not nearly so keen—I don't know whether that's so?'

'To a certain extent,' she said.

'So I'm keeping them hanging about a bit,' he said. 'So that you can have a look at the MS. first.'

'It's non-fiction, I suppose,' she said.

'A true story,' he said. 'A war story. I believe they still sell quite well?'

'Oh yes,' she said, apparently searching for fleas on her dog's broad back. 'Very well.'

'Then if I may I'll leave it with you,' he said. 'And perhaps I may call at your office tomorrow.'

'I'm afraid I'm rather busy tomorrow,' she said. 'Perhaps later this week . . . ?'

'I'll call in tomorrow on the off-chance,' he said. He moved towards the door. 'I really must apologise for having bothered you with all this tonight, but it seemed too good an opportunity to waste as I was just passing, and as you see there is a certain amount of urgency about it because of my having already got Blow interested. But I suppose you must be used to importunate authors.'

She smiled politely, following him out into the hall. Heavy steps stumped up from the basement and Jean-Claude appeared with Baldwin's coat.

'It's funny that I don't remember Anthony ever mentioning your name,' said Judith Lane.

'I only knew him slightly in England,' said Baldwin. 'We never really had much to do with each other until we went to Korea. Circumstances happened to keep us as much apart as two people in one regiment can be until then.'

She nodded, as if she found that only natural. 'You're a regular soldier?' she asked.

'I'm a barrister now,' he said, with an echo of satisfaction in his voice. 'But at the time I had signed on for an extra seven years after the end of my conscription. The seven years expired just after I got back from the prison camp in China. I quite liked the Army in many ways, but I never wanted to stay there for good. It was useful to me, though; it kept me fed for those years and I took my Bar exams in my spare time—all except the last that is, which I crammed for as soon as I came out. That was probably why I didn't see much of Anthony while we were both in London. I was working at my law all my spare time.'

He had been talking partly to cover up his embarrassment

over the struggle on which he was at the same time engaged with the midget, who was refusing to let go of his overcoat. As the highest he could reach was about on a level with Baldwin's lowest rib, it had seemed simpler to Baldwin to take the coat away from him and put it on himself, but Jean-Claude, smiling broadly, shook his head and guided Baldwin's hand into one of the sleeves. Baldwin was then in the foolish position of having his coat put on for him by a man who could only just reach above his waist, and as Jean-Claude kept a surprisingly firm hold on the collar he was forced after a moment to give in and bend his knees. Jean-Claude then with much out-blowing of garlicky breath made a great show of smoothing the shoulders and fitting the collar in exactly the right place, keeping Baldwin bent to his own level with the aid of one large hand on his shoulder.

Aware that the girl had watched this exhibition with cool pleasure, Baldwin left rather hurriedly, without shaking her hand, merely saying: 'Then I shall hope to see you tomorrow,' and walking quickly down the street towards the King's Road.

It had gone quite well, he thought as he went, but for the midget. The midget was unbearable.

A little later, Jean-Claude, who had been putting the dog out, came in with the envelope which Baldwin had left in the hall and held it out to Judith. 'You are wanting?' he asked.

She looked at him. 'It's only something he wanted me to read,' she said, after a moment. 'Leave it in the hall. I'll look at it tomorrow.' But when she went upstairs to bed, she was carrying it under her arm.

Every day there was a moment—every week-day, every working day—when her prepared glance sped between the trees of Royal Avenue to the clock tower of Chelsea Hospital, then the straight view slid sideways and the bus carried her forward. It was a ritual begun in the early days of her marriage, when the assuming of a routine had seemed not merely efficient and adult like being able to cook, but also an enchanted initiation, a form of service lovingly learnt by a religious convert. Happiness had fitted into a framework, whose removal would have taken away half her newly-established confidence, though for convention's sake she had pretended to despise it—a convention of being unconventional which it had at the time seemed important not to break. Her slight occasional complaint was also because she did not think it wise for her husband to know the full measure of her content, because she was aware of his tendency to lose interest in what was wholly his, a tendency which she never in the brief course of her married life ignored.

There was now no need for her to pretend that she derived anything but the keenest enjoyment from her morning bus ride to the office. Her code of unconventionality had long since dissolved and there was no one she had to pretend not to adore; so the morning bus usually saw her smiling over the top of her dog's large round head, looking out for each familiar landmark while her mind wallowed in an extravagant day-dream for which the rest of the day was too occupied.

Today the trees were sharply black, or rather that deep dark green which seems blacker than black and which trees usually have in the evening when the light has almost gone, and it was too misty to see the clock tower. The mist seemed a result of the temperature, like a heat haze only the opposite, rather than a rainy, or dewy, mist, for it was that very cold late February that followed the first brief signs of spring that year. Even on such a morning, a morning too on which she had something to worry about, happiness was too much a habit to be so quickly changed. The familiarities of the routine once loved for reasons now mainly removed had assumed the character almost of childhood recollections, were something like a certain corner of an otherwise unimportant yew hedge or the small patch which was the burial ground of several canaries and rabbits, intimately remembered places with a quality now of revelation about them, only that they revealed the past and not the future.

So she listened with equanimity to the conversation behind her as an elderly lady with blue hair and a neat rubicund man whom she had just rapturously greeted chattered in lively loud stage voices.

'Wimbledon!' the woman deeply fluted. 'My dear the places they choose! And I have to go to Maida Vale at eight-thirty —eight-thirty!—for The Rivals.'

'Wimbledon Common,' the man said. 'On Sunday morning and in a wig.'

'Oh they've forgotten what Sunday is,' the woman lamented. 'A wig?'

'We're supposed to be cavaliers,' said the man, with exaggerated dolefulness.

'The things they do to us,' said the woman in a satisfied tone. 'But oh, I must tell you about the water board. Without a word, without so much as one of those squalid little notes, they cut us off! Not, my dear, because we hadn't paid the bill, oh no, because they were *altering* something. And I said to the man, "If someone should be ill?" and he coolly said, "There's a temporary pump," but had they told us there was a temporary pump? Oh dear me no. Not till four o'clock in the morning did I know there was a temporary pump.'

'You spoke to him at four o'clock?'

'Not spoke to him, no,' the woman answered. 'But heard it. My dear, it was Niagara in the streets, the temporary pump. But till then from the afternoon before I might have died for want of water for all they cared.'

Their conversation rushed on and everyone listened, drawn together, rather, on the top of the bus, by their joint amusement, their joint hope that the two talkers might turn out to be famous.

'Supposing I were suddenly to turn round,' Judith thought, 'and say, "The Water Board may worry you, but I was told last night my husband was what you would call a coward and a traitor—well, that perhaps I knew, but I was told that other people knew, which was worse——" '

But as if some echo of the thought had reached her, the elderly actress was saying: 'How awfully brave, those people on the life-boat, did you see? Trying to save those sailors from the wrecked tanker. Wasn't it dreadfully sad? And did you see the captain's telegram? Lost carrying out the supreme duty of saving lives—something like that. Such a wonderful phrase, I thought, the supreme duty. It's a naval expression I suppose. Some of their messages are so wonderful, don't you think, that one reads?'

Judith felt tears ready to fill her eyes at the thought of great duties fulfilled. The fact that her late husband had evidently failed to fulfil his seemed neither here nor there: he had not needed duty, but to someone who did nothing could be more satisfying than to carry it out, and she felt a little envious of the men who had died so grandly. A sense of responsibility properly applied could be a great comfort to the applier.

The bus ride was familiar to Bertie too, and at Hyde Park Corner he scrambled from her knee some time before the bus stop. A middle-aged man in a bowler hat said, 'Good doggie, nice little bow-wow,' in a busy portentous way as they went down the stairs.

The Park Lane office of Messrs Hanescu Lane & Co. Ltd., one of the few publishing firms to have been successful since the end of the war, was inclined to arouse as a first reaction from clients a certain amount of distrust; it was unbelievably sumptuous. Baldwin Reeves, when he saw it later, had his fill of fitted carpets. They abounded, and so did flowers and filled cigarette boxes, and wildly expensive modern furniture, white telephones, beautifully bound reference books and good pictures by young little-known painters. There was only one secretary, but she abounded too.

One came first into a peacock blue room with crimson damask curtains. The carpet there had to be washed once a week by a very expensive firm of office cleaners. There was a huge vase of flowers on a gilt and ebony table, some modern Italian chairs and sofas, some low marble tables. From this room one door led to Feliks Hanescu's office and another to the room where Fisher and Miss Vanderbanks sat, beyond which was Judith's office.

The Chairman and Managing Director's room was black

and white: black carpet, white armchairs, black desk with a large white extension for telephones, black desk chair. There were black velvet curtains lined with white silk, and white Venetian blinds. The walls were white and were hung with two huge ferocious landscapes and a sketch of Hanescu's head by a famous artist. There was a small white filing cabinet with imitation Sèvres handles in one corner, and a long, low black bookcase filled with manuscripts.

Miss Vanderbank the secretary and Fisher the young man with money worked entrellised in rosebuds. Hanescu had been immovable on this point—Fisher and Miss Vanderbank were to have rosebuds or nothing, and since for Miss Vanderbank the pay was good and for Fisher the prospects, supposedly, alluring, they had of course had rosebuds. Hanescu, quite carried away by the unsuitability of it, had wanted to have gay chintz curtains and armchairs and had even suggested a Welsh dresser for keeping manuscripts in, but here he had been overruled and the curtains and carpets were in fact a serviceable dark green, and Fisher's desk, the chairs and filing cabinets were comparatively conventional, though Miss Vanderbank's typing desk was a riot of gadgets.

The argument over Judith's room had lasted for weeks. Hanescu had wanted a William Morris wallpaper, a painted green and white desk (feminine, he thought) and, suddenly, a copper Christ in a pale green alcove. In the end the walls were the colour of bull's blood, the carpet and curtains pale grey and the furniture mahogany. 'This is for the simpler authors.' Hanescu said. 'Up from the country,' and he bought a set of sporting prints for the walls.

Feliks's voice greeted Judith as she came into the office.

'I'm afraid she's in conference at the moment,' he was saying. 'Can I take a message?'

'What is it?' asked Judith.

'Oh wait a moment, I think I might be able to catch her,' Feliks said, still on the telephone. Turning to Judith, he said: 'Good morning. I'll put you through if you go to your office.'

'I'll do it here,' said Judith. 'Who is it?'

'Oh no,' said Feliks. 'It's a *private* call. Come on.' He led her through Fisher's and Miss Vanderbank's room, which was empty. 'Honey and flowers,' he said. 'A man with a voice all honey and flowers it is.'

Judith lifted the receiver and her mother-in-law asked her to tea.

'She thinks I'm common,' said Feliks, when the conversation was over.

'It's not that so much as that she fears you have no roots, which is not quite the same thing,' said Judith. 'She likes people to have roots.'

'Oh but branches too,' said Feliks. 'Wiltshire branches, Sussex branches, cadet branches, branches sinister, branches distaff. I have none. I must marry and found a dynasty. Do you suppose Miss Vanderbank would be fruitful?'

'Where are they?' Judith asked.

'I sent them both out to have coffee,' said Feliks. 'I think they're falling in love.'

Feliks Hanescu was huge. The fact was a continual source of irritation to him, for he believed that only little men were great. 'If I had been six inches smaller,' he said, 'I should have been a genius.' That was what he had wanted to be, a genius: having just missed it, he had become a personality instead.

There was nothing small about him at all, except his writing which was illegible because he had once heard that the cleverest people have the smallest writing. He had a large, dark, handsome head, yellowish bright-eyed face and hooked nose. The nose was useful to him for it enabled him when he wished to pass himself off as a Jew, which he sometimes found advantageous from the business point of view. In fact he was neither Jewish, nor, as rumour among the gullible had been known to run, of Rumanian royal blood. His father had indeed been Rumanian—a moderately successful business man who had settled in England and married, in the first flush of his enthusiasm for all that was English, a handsome Sussex farmer's daughter. When it dawned on him that this had been, socially speaking, a mistake, he at once abandoned his wife, and the young Feliks was then submitted to the care of a brisk succession of step-mothers, culled from varying social *milieux*, until Hanescu senior in his old age blissfully settled down with the jolly old daughter of an Irish peer. Feliks meanwhile had been conventionally educated at a small public school which by no means deserved the denial he usually accorded it.

Feliks Hanescu Limited had begun in 1947 in a dingy little office in John Street, Bloomsbury, lit mainly by the glowing presence of the enamoured Miss Vanderbank. Eighteen months later it was declared bankrupt. A year after it re-emerged, its reputation only slightly tarnished and all its debts discharged, owing to the death of Mr. Hanescu senior, who had left his son a modest fortune.

Feliks Hanescu had energy, talent, salesmanship, and an infinite capacity for remembering names. He also had, for the moment, a considerable unearned income. He soon acquired a reputation as an up and coming young man, and a large clientele of ex-convicts, war heroes and deep-sea divers, who, greedily pursued by other publishers, came to him partly because he often caught them before anybody else and partly because they had heard he was good at pushing sales, which was true.

It was Alastair Drudge who had first introduced him to Judith. Alastair Drudge was a plain young red-haired girl who kept Siamese cats and wrote highbrow novels. Feliks disliked her intensely, but he was anxious for his list to be more literary and she thought he adored her. She took him to a party in the Cromwell Road where he glittered and smouldered and ensnared what he hoped were all the new young writers and where someone said: 'There's Judith Fortune—you know, Edward Fortune's daughter,' and he fell in love.

To Feliks Hanescu love and sex were one and the same. Judith, bewildered, studiedly remote and actually fascinated (though this he never knew) rejected his advances. After a time he transferred them to more welcoming objectives and concentrated on conversation. If he had been asked at any time after the first tumultuous month of their acquaintance whether or not he was in love with Judith he would have sincerely denied it, but a more introspective man in his place might have said: 'Yes, a little.' Judith passed through a stage when she rather priggishly condemned him as a charlatan, and then settled down to be his greatest friend.

When she joined his firm she brought the literary tone which he now felt he needed. Her father, Edward Fortune, who had just died, had been a much respected critic, a translator of modern German literature, and a publishers' reader—a serious, learned, kind man, who had advised and been loved by a great number of the writers of his time. His wife Hilda's earnest novels still had their influence and might have had more if they had not been suddenly cut short by her early death when Judith was fifteen.

Judith herself had a critical faculty which served the firm well, and Feliks Hanescu Ltd. began to combine sensational non-fiction with the work of younger, more intellectual writers. It began to be the thing for a new writer to be published by Hanescu.

On Judith's marriage she became a partner, and with some of Anthony Lane's money and most of poor Fisher's they expanded, and moved, to a background of protests from Judith, into the new office. There the firm flourished, even though there were still times when it lived, if not from day to day, at least from month to month.

At the moment their chief hopes were pinned on a book by a white woman who had married an African chieftain, and which had been out for three days.

Judith, remembering this, asked: 'How's that awful book?'

'You mustn't despise your bread and butter,' said Feliks. 'If you mean *Love Is Not Skin Deep*. The booksellers say it's going well, though they haven't asked for more copies yet. Fisher has finally sold the Australian serial rights, after months of feverish negotiation—that's why he's treating Miss Vanderbank to coffee. They've probably gone to Gunter's to stuff themselves with cakes in celebration. So that's nearly everything sold. The film option's definite now and Peters said he thought it very likely they'd take it up. You look worried. Why?'

'Oh this and that,' said Judith.

'You should have no thises and thats,' said Feliks. 'Not when you have me.' He was standing near the window, and happening to look out he added: 'Not when you have Fisher, either, and Miss Vanderbank and that nice-looking plumpish fellow who must be a brother bun-eater.'

'Plumpish?' said Judith.

'Plumpish,' said Feliks. 'Well, they mustn't find us idling so. Stomp's coming in at twelve. I shall send him to you.'

'Who's Stomp?'

'He wrote that horribly technical book about sex,' said Feliks. 'If not Stomp, something like it. He won't be put off by me, and you're so cool with that sort of person.'

'Why on earth did you let it get to the stage of his coming in?' complained Judith.

'I'm so weak,' said Feliks, going back to his own office. 'I'm so weak and you're so strong.'

Judith sat down at her desk and waited for Baldwin Reeves.

He had not really been to Gunters, but had merely happened to cross the road at the same time as Fisher and Miss Vanderbank, and had followed them up the stairs without knowing that their destination was the same as his. When he discovered that it was, he expressed his delight in terms highly flattering to Miss Vanderbank, and asked her which was Mrs. Lane's room.

'I'll see if she's in, shall I?' said Miss Vanderbank. 'She's usually in about this time.'

'Oh don't bother, I don't need announcing,' said Baldwin.

'I think it would be better if I asked her first, if you don't mind,' said Miss Vanderbank, robustly. 'People usually make appointments you see, to see Mrs. Lane herself.' She bounced away into Judith's room.

Baldwin turned to the pale young man who was hanging awkwardly in the background. 'I seem to have been a little brash,' he said. 'Of course Mrs. Lane is very important.'

'Oh she's not *self*-important,' said the young man with

desperate earnestness. 'Not in the slightest. But she's awfully intelligent, of course, and we have to, well, in a way, protect her from people who might waste her time, if you see what I mean?'

'I see,' said Baldwin. There was always special treatment for the Lanes. This young man's voice had a familiar ring; it might have been some young subaltern of Anthony's who was speaking. Baldwin's old resentment came back to him; but with a difference, for the wife had not half Anthony's charm or looks. Anthony had commanded even from Baldwin something that was a little like love. Judith's qualities were so much less enchanting that he expected to be able to behave towards her as he really felt towards her, a thing which he had never been able to do with Anthony. At least he had given her something now which ought to have shaken her.

His first thought when he was allowed into her room was that he might have known that she wouldn't be shaken. She was as calm and indifferent as she had been yesterday: if she was a little paler it was hardly noticeable.

'I'm so sorry to burst in like this,' he began. 'Only I thought possibly early would be better than late, since you said you were rather booked up today. I say, I do like your offices.'

'Won't you sit down,' said Judith. She was sitting behind her desk, and the effect was pleasantly unusual: he could imagine new authors being favourably struck.

'I'm afraid I can't quite see your object in suggesting that we might be interested in publishing this MS.,' she said. 'I should have thought it would have been obvious that we were the last people to ask.'

'I thought you might like to see it before it appeared in the paper,' said Baldwin.

'So that it would be less of a shock?' she said. 'Perhaps you're right. You chose a rather melodramatic way of doing it.' She pushed the envelope towards him across the desk. 'Thank you for letting me see it. I don't think there is anything else I can say at the moment, is there?'

It suddenly seemed difficult to prolong the interview. Baldwin said: 'I thought perhaps you might want to know more —more than I have written I mean.'

'Is there more?' she asked. 'You have told me he was a coward, that during the famous siege he was, as you put it, "cowering" in a corner and that he was booed by his men when he emerged. You have told me that in the prison camp he made some agreement with the enemy, and that he gave away a plan to escape as a result of which two of his companions were shot, and that you all condemned him to death and hanged him. What more can there be?'

She spoke in a voice which was completely dry and cold, and yet she brought Anthony to his mind in a way which had not happened for years. Perhaps it was simply the effect of talking to someone who had known him as well as he had.

'You mustn't think,' he said, 'that all the time—after we were captured and so on—we were enemies. That was the extraordinary thing. I mean, not only had he been afraid, but, as I wrote, he was in such a panic that when the order got through to retreat he thought it was an order to stay where we were. He kept begging me to let us retreat, and I refused, because of what he told me this order had been—then when I finally found out, of course it was too late and that was why so many people were killed and the rest of us captured.'

'The people who had issued the order,' said Judith. 'Did they not wonder why it hadn't been obeyed?'

'Everything happened so quickly, you know,' said Baldwin. 'They might not have known anything about it—I honestly don't know. I had one very odd conversation with the colonel, in which I really didn't know what he was getting at, but the truth is, you see, what good would it have done to let the whole story come out, even if they did guess that something had gone wrong? Their instinct would have been to cover it up, particularly as he was dead, and particularly as he had been given such popular acclaim as a hero.'

'I suppose so,' she said.

'But as I was saying,' he went on. 'The extraordinary thing was that by the time we reached China we were all on speaking terms with him again. We'd started off by being, well, pretty contemptuous, treating him as a traitor; but you know he seemed to have so little idea himself of having done anything to be ashamed of, and then he was funny, really very funny, and somehow clowned himself out of a situation you'd have thought impossible. It was his fault we were there, and yet a week after our capture we were all laughing at his jokes, and even—and this was amazing—vying with each other for his good opinion. He seemed so detached, and could at the same time be so attractive, that one longed to make an impression on him. I think he was tremendously relieved that we were out of danger, and also he expected to be free again in a few weeks, and it made him so cheerful that he was even helpful to the rest of us—carried things for people, helped them on the march, all with a sort of carefree condescension; and then his talk was brilliant and he laughed and played harmless practical jokes on the guards so that even they were amused by him. Of course he'd had more rest than we had in the last few days.'

'I suppose he wasn't at all worried about what would happen when he did get back?' she asked.

'I don't think so,' he said. 'We didn't say anything about it for a long time, but later I asked him what he thought would happen to him. He clasped his brow, you know, and groaned, and said how terrible it was; but then he said well, perhaps it would be all right in the end. There were two things I think that prevented him from really worrying. One was his curious fatalism, and the other was his confidence that the power over people that his own charm gave him would never let him down. You might think they'd be contradictory, but the point was that I really don't think he ever made the slightest effort to charm people, so that in a way he could be fatalistic about that too.'

'His charm and his family,' she said. 'Perhaps they even might have got him out of it.'

Her slight smile surprised him. Somehow they were discussing her dead husband as if he had really been Baldwin's greatest friend, as if they had both loved him and were now in admiration and wonder trying to remember for sentimentality's sake exactly how much. This was not what he had meant.

'Then we got to the prison camp, as I wrote,' he said. 'And then things weren't so good—it's all in there. . . .' he gesticulated towards the envelope on her desk. 'And then there was this fantastic trial in the middle of the night, with all the inmates of the prison there, and he was sentenced.'

'Why was he hanged?' she asked. 'And not shot, I mean.'

'We had no guns,' he said. She was far calmer than he was, and he resented that furiously. If she had shown signs of suffering he might have told her that the verdict had not been unanimous, that there had been one vote against it and that it had been his; but as it was he was not going to tell her; it was far too intimate a confession. For the moment he hated her—for being herself, for being Anthony—he hardly knew which.

'Then you didn't mind my publishing this story?' he said.

'Mind?' she asked. 'I suppose I can't stop you, though I am not quite certain why you want to do it.'

'You are in the literary business,' he smiled unpleasantly. 'You should know the high fees newspapers pay for a good story. This is a very good story—a popular hero, still in the public mind, proved a coward and a traitor? No one's forgotten him you know—practically every day there's something about him in some paper or other, some public speech, people are always telling me how lucky I was to have known him. I don't make much money. Unlike your late husband, I have no private income, nor have I a powerful family. I am a self-made, or perhaps I should say self-making, man. I am at the moment in great need of money.'

'But, surely, couldn't you make it in some other way?' She still looked bewildered.

'Possibly,' he said. 'But this seems, really, the easiest. Unless, of course someone were to pay me not to.'

After a moment she laughed.

'I see, I see, I see,' she said. 'D'you know honestly that aspect of the affair hadn't occurred to me at all. What an innocent I must be. I have been wondering all the time why you came to tell me this, and I never thought of the simple obvious answer, blackmail.'

'Blackmail,' he nodded.

'Surely you should say, "That's an ugly word",' she said.

'Why?' he asked.

'Don't they in detective stories?' she said.

'I hope this is not going to be a detective story,' he said.

'No, I don't suppose a detective would be much good,' she said. 'I might try, though.'

'You might,' he said. 'But then of course I should be forced to reveal the story, which I may say is neatly typed out in a sealed envelope in my office, together with the names of the other eight witnesses, and can be sent off by my secretary to a journalist I know at a moment's notice.'

'But I thought you told me you had already sold it to the *Sunday News.*'

'That was an exaggeration,' he said. 'I had merely sounded them, without committing myself or revealing the story.'

'I see,' she said. 'How you have thought it out. How extraordinary.'

'Well, there it is, you see,' he said. 'I've no doubt in a few years I shall be making money—I fully intend to make a great deal—but for the moment as I say, a few hundred would be very welcome.'

'A few hundred.'

'I had thought of five, for a start. At first I hoped for more, but I understand your marriage settlement from the Lanes wasn't as generous as it might have been.'

'How did you find that out?'

'Oh, I asked about, you know. But I imagine this firm brings in something, or does Mr. Hanescu take all that?'

'I don't get much,' she said. 'I certainly haven't got £500 just like that.'

Baldwin shook his head sympathetically. 'Indeed, who has these days?' he said, sadly. 'Still, no doubt you'll be able to raise it.'

'Well, wait a minute,' she said. 'I may not want to. I may not think it worth it. I don't think I do, from my own point of view. My feelings for my late husband were not based on the fact that the public at large believed him to be a hero—their thinking him a traitor won't distress me.'

'His family?' asked Baldwin.

'How d'you know that I care at all what they feel?' she said.

'I don't,' he replied. 'If you tell me you don't I shall with a clear conscience take my story to the *News* tomorrow.'

'May I have some time to think it over?' she asked.

'Certainly,' he said, standing up. 'Let's say you'll ring me up tomorrow evening.'

'The next day,' she said.

'All right, we'll make it Wednesday,' he said generously. 'Here's my number.' He pulled a card from his pocket. 'Of course if you decide to go away without getting in touch with me, or anything like that, I shall have to sell the story—purely to pay my rent.'

'I'll ring you up on Wednesday evening about six,' she said.

'Right,' he moved to the door. 'I'm sorry about this but I'm sure you understand my position.'

'Oh yes, I understand it,' she said. She watched him without expression as he went out of the room. At the door, he looked back and would have said 'Good-bye', but after a moment's pause he left without saying anything more.

He thought, going down the stairs and out into Park Lane, 'I am a blackmailer'. He had not known, when he had followed Fisher and Miss Vanderbank into the office a short time ago, or at least had not known for certain, that it was in such a capacity that he would emerge. He was not yet quite sure how he liked it, but after all he had wanted to be ruthless and he had wanted to make money, and it looked as though he was going to be able to do both.

Judith went to the office early the next morning, and found Feliks in her room, looking through her letters.

'My own are so boring,' he said.

'Supposing,' Judith said, taking off her coat. 'Supposing, by

34

any chance, *Love Is Not Skin Deep*—I mean the book really did sell—supposing——'

'Hang your coat up nicely,' said Feliks, picking it up from the chair where she had thrown it. 'How you do let down the tone of this office.' And he carried the coat out to the cupboard in the next room.

When he had come back and shut the door, Judith said: 'I want to borrow some money from the firm.'

'You've been gambling,' he said, sitting on the edge of her desk.

'No, I haven't,' she answered.

'But you, so frugal, need money?' he asked. 'I thought you were all right—you were saying so only the other day.'

'I know, Feliks,' she said. 'But this is something unexpected that I've suddenly got to pay.'

'If it's an abortion,' said Feliks, 'I'd much rather adopt it.'

'I don't know how much an abortion costs,' said Judith. 'But I should think this is more, I don't know.'

'How much?'

'£500,' she said.

'Oh God yes,' he said. 'Much more. Well, all right.'

'£500 is what I've got to pay,' she said. 'I can manage about £150 myself. That leaves £350.'

'Take £200 from the firm and I'll lend you the rest,' said Feliks. 'Only don't tell anyone and pay me back before the firm.'

'Thank you very much,' she said. 'I'll pay you back quite soon, really, and the firm. I'll give banker's orders.'

'Don't worry,' he said. 'Don't worry at all. I hate you to be worried. It makes you snappish in the office and then you humiliate me in front of Miss Vanderbank. You're all right, aren't you?'

'Oh yes, I'm all right,' she answered, looking down.

'And don't let anyone know about that £150,' he went on. 'Heaven knows what would become of my reputation if that got out.' It was one of his affectations to pretend to be pathologically mean: some of the stories about this supposed failing were very funny, whether told by his friends, his enemies, or himself.

'I'd better give it you now.' He got out his cheque book, made a few minute indecipherable marks on a cheque and gave it her.

When he went through the other room he said to Fisher and Miss Vanderbank: 'I've just given Mrs. Lane a cheque for £150.'

The pale face and the pink looked up at the same time and laughed obediently.

3

He said he had to have it in cash. She thought at first this might be merely a pretext for forcing her to hand it over in person, so that he could extract the fullest pleasure from the exercise of his power over her; but later it occurred to her that it must be to avoid leaving any record of his having received the money.

She had already considered carefully whether there could be any hope of catching him out, had imagined policemen concealed behind the curtains and springing out to arrest him at the moment the money changed hands, but these ideas struck her as so melodramatic and unreal that it seemed impossible they should ever become fact. Besides she had the money now, and she had come to think that perhaps she did somehow owe it to someone for her husband's having failed as he had.

She was in this fatalistic frame of mind when she went with £500 to meet him at a coffee bar in the King's Road. She had asked for an extra week's grace in which to collect the money, and by the end of the week she was feeling depressed and rather ill.

It was not that she consciously thought about it so very much—the having to pay £500 and the reason for it—as that all the time it was at the back of her mind, or, as it rather seemed, on the top of her mind, weighing down on everything beneath it, ready to slip into her conscious thoughts the moment there should be room. She had not yet much questioned it, had so far more or less calmly accepted it as simply something else which Anthony had imposed on her, for there had in the past been other lesser situations not altogether dissimilar. In fact the chief emotion aroused by this talk about him, apart from a vague and dreadful sense of brooding doom, of an imminent outburst of either events or emotions, had been one of renewed longing that he might have been alive, anyhow, however disgracefully.

It was six o'clock and the place was not crowded. Baldwin Reeves was sitting in a corner beneath a rather dusty orange tree (it was all Spanish) and looked, particularly in contrast to the group of grubby students who were sitting at the next table, surprisingly proper and pleasant. She had remembered him as fat, untidy and overbearing, and now he looked neat, intelligent and friendly.

When he saw her he got up, folding his evening paper, smiling—they might have been new friends about to spend a delightful evening together.

He, too, was surprised, because she was looking far more sophisticated than when he had last seen her. In a short fur coat which Anthony had given her, a fashionably tweedy dress and high heels, and with her pretty dog, she looked much more interesting than he could have hoped—people turned to look at her.

As he had thought it would, it made a difference. Perhaps this needn't be the brisk formal encounter he had envisaged, after all.

She, however, seemed to expect that sort of meeting, for she had no sooner sat down than she pulled a bulky envelope from her bag and slapping it down on the table in front of him said: 'D'you want to count it?'

'What will you have?' he asked as if she had not spoken.

'To drink? Oh, nothing thank you.'

'Please do,' he said. 'I thought you'd be late, so I ordered this huge mug of chocolate which is already making me feel sick. Do have something.'

'No, really, I won't, thank you,' she said. 'I must go.'

'Have some fruit juice, do,' he said. 'It's really quite good. Melon or something?'

'Oh, well, some lemon then,' she said, feeling that she had conceded something much more important and leaning back gloomily.

'Thank you,' he said, and ordered it. 'Yes, I thought women were always late,' he went on.

'Oh, are they?' she said, indifferently.

There were women, in his experience, who liked to be constantly reminded of their sex, others who pretended to find that insulting: she seemed to belong to the latter category. It made no difference, in his experience, they were all much the same fundamentally; but one might as well observe their whims. He did not then follow up his last remark, but said instead: 'Tell me how you acquired your dwarf.'

'He's not a dwarf, he's a midget,' she said. 'They're different.'

'Oh, are they?' he said. 'And he's a French midget?'

'Yes,' she said. 'He's got a horrid accent in French too.'

'Is that some regional dialect?'

'I don't know,' she said. 'I found him in Paris.'

'Found him?' asked Baldwin.

She smiled. 'In a way,' she said.

As she remained silent, he said, 'Do tell me about it.'

'Oh, well,' she said, looking away. 'I can't be bothered somehow.'

Perhaps the midget was her lover after all. Baldwin wanted to know; but looking at her blank profile he decided to drop the subject and make inquiries elsewhere.

'Have a bun or something,' he said.

She refused, but he, with evident interest, selected for himself two creamy *pâtisseries* and brought them to the table.

'You'll get fatter,' she said coldly.

'I am rather fat, aren't I?' he said. 'But I don't mind being a little fat as long as it's not too much. I don't think it really detracts from a man's appearance, do you, as long as he's healthy?

Do I look very fat at first sight, I mean would people describe me to each other, d'you suppose, as "that fat man"? It's hard to tell how one strikes people. Did you think me fat when you first saw me?'

'Fattish,' she said.

'But d'you think I ought to try to get thinner?' he asked. 'Should I diet, d'you think?'

She looked at him in surprise as he waited with apparent eagerness for her answer. Then she said: 'I asked you if you wanted to count the money.'

He looked disappointed. 'You're right, of course,' he said. 'What does it matter how fat I am? No, I don't want to count it. Let's have dinner together. I'll take you somewhere—we'll see how much we can spend.'

'I think you're very odd,' she said. 'I must go now.' She stood up, attracted the attention of Bertie, whose lead she had let go and who was being fed on lumps of sugar by an enraptured old lady, and began to walk away.

'I hope you have a good dinner,' she said.

A rough wind whipped her as she strode along the King's Road, but even so she thought, approaching her house, that she could not yet go back there, speak to Jean-Claude, eat, read, think. She turned left down Smith Street, finding the wind less violent once she was round the corner, saying to the dog: 'Come on, Bertie, we're going for a walk. You're so lazy,' for he knew where they were and was straining at his lead in the direction of their house, remembering the cats that lurked behind it and his duty as he conceived it endlessly to bark at them.

She had forgotten, however, that Burton Court would be shut. She had thought they might have run in there, thrown sticks and shouted, to relieve the oppression of her mood. She walked instead on and on, quite quickly now, and down Swan Walk and to the river.

There, still bossed about by the wind, she paused and leant on the wall of the deserted Embankment, seeing through the dark night the vague river swirling and saying at last with furious feeling: 'I hate him, I hate him.'

She spoke not of Baldwin Reeves but of her dead husband, and the familiarity of all her sensations, stronger though they were than most she had felt before, made her sob as she said it.

It was a pattern she had been used to—the outrageous demand, the meek obedience to it, the ensuing useless rage. Life had always been like that with Anthony.

After a few incidents, a few of his own particular betrayals, she had thought: 'This must be the end of everything—how can I feel the same afterwards?' but each time it had been anything but the end and each time she had felt exactly the same afterwards. Later she had come to believe what had at first seemed to her odd and rather degrading, that love was not always based on a similarity of principles, and that it was possible genuinely to love and even at times to admire someone whom one could seldom, if ever, respect. She had also occasionally recognised in herself an emotion approaching a sort of enjoyment in quietly submitting herself to the distresses, inconveniences and humiliations which his behaviour from time to time caused her.

She knew then this evening above the dark winter river that her fury would soon fade, but it made her for the moment more rather than less resentful. It was little comfort to know that an hour or two later love would have changed her mind.

4

When Judith announced her engagement to Anthony Lane, her paternal aunt, who was rather common, congratulated her on being about to marry 'into a place'.

'I always knew you were meant for something special,' she wrote. 'In spite of your poor mother.'

There was land, there were tenants, employees, villagers, dogs, portraits, plantations. To that extent Aunt Edith Fortune would have been satisfied; but the house itself might have surprised her. It looked more like a church than anything else, a dilapidated, deconsecrated, church with large haphazard windows later added. It had started as a pele tower, embattled, crenellated, and machicolated by licence granted in 1280 to Humphry Lane, a Wensleydale farmer. Subsequent generations had added to it until in about 1690, the family prospering, a grander house was begun a mile away, and with its beauty as their setting the Lanes went on from strength to strength. In 1863 the house caught fire, no one knew how, and was burnt to the ground.

The old couple of the time moved into the tower, which was then a farm, and the shell of the other house was left crumbling gently, and not without a bizarre beauty, in the middle of its grand abandoned gardens.

There had never been quite the money or the time or the energy to rebuild it; and now there doubtless never would be, not only because of the turning away of the times from that sort of building but because there were no young Lanes.

The tower house would have looked less bleak had there been a lovely garden, but though the deserted garden of the ruined house a mile away flourished, this one had never been a success, and the Wensleydale moors were everywhere the eye could see.

Judith from the first had accorded the house—Harris was its name—her unswerving loyalty. There was no particular reason for this; the house seemed to her simply to demand it, the house and the old man and his stern feared daughter-in-law.

The real church was in fact two miles away, and they drove to it every Sunday, Sir Ralph Lane, Mrs. Lane, and when she was there—which, the winter Sunday after she had given Baldwin Reeves £500, she was—Judith. They used to walk but then the old man got beyond it.

Mr. Wardle, the vicar, had been there now for twenty years, and the excesses of his youth were far behind him. There had been excesses, of a sort, or so Mrs. Lane would have called them. They had included incense, and bells, and acolytes, and very odd ideas about transubstantiation.

Mrs. Lane had been in Moscow when Mr. Wardle, the former incumbent having died, had been inducted at All Saints, Ribblethwaite. She had returned with her young son after her husband's death in 1936 to find that what she called 'decent English Morning Prayer' had been superseded under the new regime by something called 'Sung Eucharist'. This frankly Popish ceremony involved the co-operation of little Willie Judd and even littler Johnny Wilson as incense swingers, bell ringers and general antic-performers (this at least was how Mrs. Lane saw it) and necessitated the presence of a much enlarged choir (and therefore much worse, for how could more than six little boys be expected to sing in tune in a village of only seven hundred?) which was kept breathlessly busy throughout the service, alternately chanting, genuflecting and nudging one another—sometimes to prompt, sometimes to snigger.

It must be admitted that quite a large proportion of the congregation enjoyed it. There was more to watch, and though the services were inclined to be rather long it made a nice break when Mr. Wardle changed his vestments in the middle, helped by Willie and Johnny, and all that chanting, though a bit doleful, made a change, and of course the new service did include the Communion, killing as it were two birds with one stone.

On the other hand, a great many people were shocked. It was not at all what they were used to, and they doubted, most of them, with a good deal of head-shaking and mouth-pursing, whether it were right. One or two in fact almost considered going over to the Baptists and taking the bus ten miles to Thorpedale every Sunday, but fortunately Mrs. Lane came back in time to render this drastic course unnecessary.

Her first reaction was that the man must be a Socialist. This was not as illogical as it might seem because for Mrs. Lane religion and class were very closely connected. The Church of England, the Conservative Party and the Landed Gentry were the articles of her faith. Anathema to her were atheists, socialists and, equally, common people with no idea of their places and fast people. That is to say, respectful villagers were on one's side, factory workers and the urban lower middle classes were not; good County families were, worldly dukes and people who spent too long in the south of France were not. She had retained this creed unshaken through several years of more or less cosmopolitan life.

Mr. Wardle, therefore, this brash newcomer (probably an atheist too since he was making such a mockery of religion) must be taught his place. It was not a short struggle, for Mr. Wardle, though weak and sentimental, was also obstinate, nor did he at first realise the strength of his opponent; but in the end, and after some sensible advice from the Rural Dean, he capitulated. Decent English Morning Prayer had come back. The only remaining difference of opinion was over the Creed, which Mr. Wardle sang: on this as on every other Sunday Mrs. Lane's deep voice could be heard through the slightly ragged chanting of the rest of the congregation, firmly speaking out her faith.

She was wearing her church tweeds. They were purplish and though well cut had an air about them of immemoriality. She wore them on Sundays all through the winter, with a fur coat over them on the coldest of days; and in the summer there was a grey coat and skirt which took their place. The unvarying nature of what she wore helped to make going to church the ritual it was at Harris, a ritual about which Anthony had always complained, but which Judith, for whom it was unlike anything she had known before, never ceased to observe with curious enjoyment.

With the tweeds went a felt hat from Lincoln Bennett, bought in 1929, three years after her marriage.

As a matter of fact, Mrs. Lane dressed extremely well, for though some of her clothes were like her tweeds, old and indomitable, seeming to have come from a more privileged age, to be surviving in order defiantly to say, like the old reactionaries they were: '*Then* we knew what quality was,' there were also others. The first time Judith had met her future mother-in-law, Mrs. Lane had asked her to tea at Claridges where she was staying, and had greeted her in exquisite black with diamonds, looking with her white hair and young face immeasurably distinguished. They had had tea and talked politely and Judith had missed not one of Mrs. Lane's gentle meanings. Judith had enjoyed the encounter, but had had no more idea then than she had now of what Mrs. Lane really thought of her.

Mr. Wardle was not encouraged to make long sermons, and Sir Ralph as they emerged from the damp cold church into the dry cold air remarked that the service had taken fifty-one minutes. Everything he did was timed, because he liked timing things. In the same way he would spend hours over his personal accounts, which he entered in the most complicated possible way in several enormous ledgers, not because he was interested to know what he had spent but because he liked doing accounts. In fact they were so complicated that they were often hopelessly inaccurate, and since he had an unshakable faith in his own calculations he was in a continual state of acrimonious correspondence with his bank manager.

Outside the church they had to wait while Miss Kennedy talked to Mrs. Lane. This happened every Sunday, too, except of course when Miss Kennedy went away, but that was very seldom. Miss Kennedy had huge legs and wore all sorts of gay woolly caps and gloves. She ran the Women's Institute, the Mother's Union, the village Conservative Party and the British Legion.

'Perhaps she has designs on Mr. Wardle,' said Judith as she and Sir Ralph walked ahead down the path.

'It's Dudgeon she fancies,' said Sir Ralph. 'She was Liberal till he came along.' Dudgeon was the constituency's Conservative agent.

'But he's so hairy,' objected Judith.

'That's what appeals to her,' said Sir Ralph. 'That's how they like them. Eh, Vicar?' Mr. Wardle was standing at the gate shaking hands with those of his parishioners as could not sidle past without this greeting. 'Isn't that so, Vicar, um?' said Sir Ralph. 'They like them hairy, eh?'

'Yes, indeed, Sir Ralph,' replied Mr. Wardle, confidently but at a loss. 'In this weather particularly, no doubt. And how long is Mrs. Anthony staying? Back tonight? Ah, dear me, yes, dear me.' He stood awkwardly clasping and unclasping his hands, radiating a Christian goodwill which he had never learnt to express, until Mrs. Lane came up, remarked that the congregation was decreasing again and drove her father-in-law and daughter-in-law briskly away in her new Jaguar.

'Have you ever heard of someone called Baldwin Reeves?' asked Judith in the car quite suddenly.

'Baldwin Reeves?' repeated her mother-in-law. 'Wasn't he a friend of Anthony's?'

'Oh, then you've met him?' Judith said.

'My dear, why look so amazed?' said Mrs. Lane. 'I used to see a lot of them all at one time, you know, when I had the flat and they were all at Wellington Barracks. I can't particularly remember meeting that one, only I remember the name because it was unusual. Wasn't he the one that wasn't quite a gentleman?'

'What's his name?' Sir Ralph asked from the back seat. 'What's the fellow's name? What did you say?'

'Baldwin Reeves, Fa,' said Mrs. Lane, in the tone of reproof she automatically adopted when speaking to the old man.

Her husband Geoffrey had called him Fa and so had Geoffrey's silly sister Kate who had married an American millionaire; now only she used the childish name, making it sound each time as if she said it out of spite. 'A friend of Anthony's,' she went on.

'I should hardly have thought he was a friend,' said Judith. 'He struck me as being anything but that.'

'Fatuous name,' said Sir Ralph. 'Bad enough as a surname. Baldwin—oh, well, I suppose you'll be calling your boy Macmillan, Judith. You'd better hurry or it'll be Gaitskell—ha-ha, Gaitskell. Oh, well, ha-ha, Baldwin. I like that.'

'Judith is not married, Fa,' said Mrs. Lane, icily.

'I know,' said Sir Ralph, tetchily. 'I know that. You don't have to tell me that. I know perfectly well all about it. I'm not a moron.'

'Perhaps he was called after the kings of Jerusalem,' said Judith.

'He got into the regiment in the war I believe,' said Mrs. Lane. 'No, I don't think Anthony did see much of him.'

'I met him the other day,' said Judith. 'That is, he came to see me. He was in Korea.'

Mrs. Lane's fine nostrils quivered slightly.

'Really?'

'Yes, and in the prison camp.'

After a little silence, Mrs. Lane turned to look at Judith then smiled at her, then, looking again at the road, put a hand for a moment on her knee and said: 'You must tell me all about it.'

In moments when they were sharing emotions about Anthony they were quite close: if those moments were to be sacrificed they might find themselves almost strangers.

At Harris Judith's secret knowledge seemed more important than it had in London; for she herself had already known a good deal about her husband's faults, but here she was surrounded by reminders that other people had apparently not known, and it made her look at them in a new light, as one looks at an ill person after a little talk in the passage with the doctor. As one can hardly believe that the patient sitting up in bed with books and flowers and grapes can really be ignorant of the evil already destroying him, so Judith wondered that the woman beside her could have failed to notice the cancer in the cherished body of her family.

For her family—first her husband and then her son—had certainly always been the reason for her existence. It was to her devotion in fact that many of his friends had ascribed Geoffrey Lane's rather unexpected marriage—that and of course her beauty.

Geoffrey Lane had been brilliant, so much so that to Judith he was hardly more than a fable. Clever, handsome, rich, his memory seemed to her that of someone always immensely privileged. He had died young, of cancer, when he was Minister in Moscow.

Though she had never got on well with her father-in-law, Grizelda Lane had come to live at Harris, partly no doubt because it would one day be Anthony's. Anthony had grown up there, and it was one of Mrs. Lane's blindnesses, whether wilful or otherwise, that she had failed to recognise his dislike of the place.

The house, all the same, still held the relics of his childhood. His nursery, untenanted, still housed a lonely rocking-horse; his battered books filled a landing staircase; and downstairs where the coats were kept was still an assortment of scarves and odd caps, Wellington boots and once loved, now meaningless, sticks and stones.

The chief relic, of course, was Nanny, who knew the whole story from the beginning, and who had stood by her bereaved mistress with an aggressive staunchness which had easily withstood Sir Ralph's early attempts to get rid of her. He had given up hope now of her ever leaving. Only occasionally he would say a little wistfully: 'Ah, Nanny, whatever shall we do without you when you go?' but since she was nearly as old as he was, his thoughts might have been of her death, which was certainly more likely than her dismissal.

Nanny's frustrated instincts, which were presumably responsible for most of her gloominess, were given their only outlet by Judith's dog, on whom she lavished in almost pathological profusion the devotion which rightly belonged to a Lane baby. Bertie, of course, having more wit and less supervision than a baby, lost no opportunity of turning this emotion into food, and came back to London after every visit to Harris in a state of liverish rotundity.

This particular Sunday morning, however, he had not been clever enough to avoid being plunged into a bath as soon as his owner had left for church (Nanny always went to 'early' and walked all the way). They came back to find him sitting very fluffily in front of the fire eating chocolate biscuits and wearing a blue ribbon round his neck.

'Oh, Nanny, d'you think ribbons, really?' Judith said.

'He likes to look nice,' said Nanny. 'Of course, I can take it off if you don't want him to have it. I only thought it would be nice for him to be nice and clean and looking nice, but of course, if you want me to take it off. . . .'

'Oh, no, no, of course not. He looks lovely,' said Judith. 'I only didn't want him to look too sissy.' She sat down beside him.

'Oh, well, if you want me to take it off. . . .' said Nanny.

'Oh, no,' said Judith. 'Don't let's take it off.'

'He doesn't think he looks sissy, do you, my duck?' said Nanny. 'But, of course, if you want me to take it off. . . .'

'What train did you say you were catching, Judith?' Sir Ralph fortunately broke in.

'The seven-ten,' answered Judith. There was only one train on Sunday evening, but Sir Ralph never failed to show the liveliest interest in the time of its departure.

'The seven-ten, ah, yes,' he said. 'Seven-ten is it? And that gets you up at about—what—eleven-thirty I suppose?'

'Yes, about that,' said Judith.

'About eleven-thirty?' said Sir Ralph. 'Like me to look it up for you? Make quite sure of the time?'

'Yes, please,' said Judith kindly.

He went to fetch the time-table and when he came back and found her alone he said, surprisingly: 'This fellow Reeves. Nice fellow?'

'Not very, no,' said Judith.

'You know,' said Sir Ralph. 'Your mother-in-law. She was very devoted to Anthony.'

'I know,' said Judith.

'Wouldn't like to hear anything anybody might have said who wasn't so fond of him, you know,' said Sir Ralph. 'Take it hard.'

'Oh, I know,' said Judith looking at him. 'I wouldn't tell her —anything of that sort. . . .'

But his eyes went quickly back to his Bradshaw.

'Seven-ten. Yes, here we are,' he said. 'Sundays only, that's it. Only two stops—King's Cross eleven-thirty-three. Now that's quite quick you know. The eleven-ten train on week-days takes longer I think.' He flicked back the pages. 'Now let's see.'

Judith said nothing, seeing that he was determined to return to minutiae; but it was interesting, she thought, that he should have noticed in what she had said about Baldwin Reeves, or in her voice as she said it, something that Mrs. Lane had evidently quite missed.

Feliks had found a princess. He could talk of nothing else.

'Another one?' Judith said. 'But look at Curtseys and Cuirasses. Look at that awful king.'

'My dear,' said Feliks. 'This one is twenty years younger than Anna Sophia, thirty times more intelligent than the king. And she can write. I asked her for a synopsis on Saturday and here it is this morning.'

Judith took the three pages of adventurous typing which he was brandishing.

'I suppose you promised her a contract on this,' she said.

'If we liked it,' said Feliks. 'If we liked it. She's penniless of course. Read it, Judith, read it. All that stuff about the Kaiser and the story about Curzon. Do admit.'

'You sound as if you had a good Saturday to Monday,' said Judith, who resented the rather inept Nancy Mitford-isms which were likely to result from his smarter week-ends.

He had been staying with one of his most useful clients, Lord Sanderson, whose father (a Lloyd George creation) had among other things built an enormous house in Surrey in the shape of a four-leaved clover. There the present peer entertained with appropriate lavishness, and there Feliks Hanescu, bright-eyed and attentive, was often to be seen 'picking up' as he put it 'threads'.

'No, but Judith, really she's quite fun, this one,' said Feliks, adding encouragingly, 'She lives with a window-cleaner.'

'A window-cleaner?' said Judith. 'How d'you know?'

'George told me, after she'd gone,' said Feliks. 'Awfully handsome, apparently. He was cleaning windows one day, she took a fancy to him, asked him in—and he never got away again. Even you must admit that's quite an achievement for a woman of fifty-two with no money at all and a very nasty house.'

'Well, but she's not going to write about the window-cleaner, is she?' said Judith.

'A really horrid house,' Feliks went on, seeing her interest was nonetheless aroused. 'And she takes in lodgers, but such nice ones, she told me—an Obolenski, such a handsome boy, a Lichtenstein, and a second cousin of King Farouk's first wife, *faute de mieux*, as she puts it. No, but Judith seriously, she has been quite grand, and she does know all these people, and I do think she'd sell.'

'You think she'd look good on the list,' said Judith. 'I know that's what it is. Well, let her write a bit first, that's all I ask, a chapter or two.'

'Oh, certainly, she can do that,' said Feliks.

He went back into his office saying: 'Get me her number, darling, would you?' to Miss Vanderbank, and Judith went on into her own room.

The telephone rang, and the voice she heard when she answered seemed for some reason so familiar that she expected it to be someone she knew much better than Baldwin Reeves.

'What about lunch?' he said.

'Lunch?' she repeated.

'Yes, today,' he said. 'I'll pick you up.'

'I'm afraid I can't possibly have lunch with you,' said Judith, coldly.

'Tomorrow,' he said. 'Oh, no, tomorrow's no good. Wednesday?'

'I'm afraid not,' said Judith.

'Thursday?' he said.

'No, I'm sorry,' said Judith. 'I am afraid I can't have lunch with you,' and she put the receiver down.

She looked into the next room. 'Polly, would you mind not putting that man through again. His name's Baldwin Reeves. I don't want to speak to him.'

'All right,' said Miss Vanderbank, writing down the name in her huge irregular hand.

Judith had no idea what his motives could be in ringing her up. Did it mean that he already wanted more money? Could he seriously imagine that she would accept his invitation?

Apparently he did, for a few days later he rang her up at

home with a similar request. Again she put the receiver down, and after that she let Jean-Claude answer the telephone. The next week Miss Vanderbank told her that a literary agent she knew wanted to speak to her, but when she lifted the receiver it was Baldwin Reeves.

'Oh, for God's sake,' she said. 'What is the point of this?'

'I simply want you to have lunch with me,' he said. 'Wouldn't it be simpler if you did?'

'I don't want to have lunch or anything else with you ever,' said Judith petulantly.

Not long after that he walked into the office, asked which was Mrs. Lane's room, and before Miss Vanderbank could stop him strode masterfully past her and confronted Judith.

Judith was discussing children's books with a shy bearded man, who wore sandals, gave the appearance of being intensely intellectual and was in fact the author of a series of books for children from two to six on agricultural implements. *Tommy the Tractor* had been the first. In front of Judith now was *Miranda the Mower*, just out, and on the author's knee his latest manuscript *Herbert the Hedgecutter*.

'So sorry to disturb you,' shouted Baldwin, gaily. 'Do go on. Pay no attention to me—I'm afraid I'm horribly early. I'll just sit down here very quietly—I'm sure Mr. . . . . I'm afraid I don't know your name? . . . won't mind?'

'Oh no, no, not at all, so sorry, Graham Wood's the name, just leaving,' said the author who spoke very quickly.

'Would you mind waiting outside?' said Judith, without looking up from her desk.

'Oh, but the other room seemed so full of activity. I should hate to disturb it,' said Baldwin. 'And if Mr. Wood really doesn't mind. . . .'

'Oh no, no not at all, just leaving,' said Mr. Wood.

'I'd rather you waited in there if you don't mind,' said Judith going towards the door to open it.

Baldwin laughingly interposed himself. 'No, no, I want to see you at work,' he said. 'Please don't make me go.'

'Oh please, not on my account, just leaving, luncheon

engagement, business all done, just leaving,' said Mr. Wood.

Defeated, Judith went back to her desk.

'I think we had just finished,' she said stiffly to Mr. Wood. 'I'll keep this one, and you'll think over the idea for the other series, won't you?'

'Yes yes yes, indeed,' he rose uncertainly to his feet, then bobbed down again to extract a neatly rolled plastic mackintosh from under his chair. 'By all means, yes yes, and then the other small point will be I know, your usual promptitude, I'm sure, yes rather.'

'I'll remind the accountant,' said Judith.

'Oh many thanks, many many thanks, no don't see me out, good-bye good-bye, good day sir, good day. . . .' Mr. Wood bowed himself out.

Baldwin shut the door behind him.

'I hope all your clients are as eager to please,' he said.

'What are you doing here?' said Judith.

'I've come to take you out to lunch.'

'I'm afraid I can't have lunch with you.'

'You haven't any other engagement—I asked your charming secretary.' (He had not in fact done this).

Judith sighed. 'I don't want to have lunch with you and I can think of no conceivable reason why you should want to have lunch with me.'

'Is it so unusual?' he asked. 'For people to want to have lunch with you?'

'It's unprecedented,' she said. 'For someone in your position.'

'Good,' he said. 'I think that's an admirable reason why we should do it. Come on, I've got a taxi waiting.' He opened the door.

'Ah, this must be Mr. Hanescu. Didn't we meet once with Gavin Miller?'

Feliks, who prided himself on his memory, said: 'Of course, in the House of Lords. Have you seen him lately?'

'Yes, I see a good deal of him,' said Baldwin. 'Now there's a man whose life story you should get.'

52

'We've tried,' said Feliks. 'Like most publishers in London. I wish you'd use your influence.'

'Oh, my influence is negligible,' said Baldwin. 'But I love using it.'

Judith went to get her coat, with a vague idea that she might slip out before they noticed her, but she returned to find them sitting in the front office, drinking sherry. Her other hope, which had been to make some sort of appeal to Feliks, faded when she saw the friendliness with which they were already treating each other.

'Sherry, my dear?' Feliks asked her.

'No, thank you.'

'Oh, well, I expect you want to get off to your lunch,' said Feliks, getting to his feet. 'What am I doing darling?' he shouted to Miss Vanderbank. 'Talk it all over with Judith,' he added to Baldwin. 'She's the one who makes all the decisions. He's full of ideas for us, Judith.'

'Of course I shall demand an enormous cut,' said Baldwin.

'We always give enormous cuts,' said Feliks. 'That's why everyone loves us.'

Miss Vanderbank approached, as discreetly as anyone could who was carrying an ostentatiously large diary.

'Ah yes,' said Feliks, glancing at it. 'I'm off into the fabulous world of films in ten minutes. It makes publishing seem so genteel. Well, good-bye, have a lovely lunch. What about writing yourself? You do a bit of journalism, don't you?'

'I've got a wonderful idea for a detective story,' said Baldwin. 'I've been meaning to write it for months.'

'Write it, my dear fellow, write it,' said Feliks, and disappeared into his office.

'Well, we must be off,' said Baldwin, rolling his eyes appreciatively at Miss Vanderbank who blushed. 'Come along.'

Downstairs he hailed a taxi.

'I thought you had one waiting,' said Judith.

'I was lying,' he said. 'The Caprice,' he added, to the driver.

'Oh no,' said Judith, 'I have to be back very early. Can't we just have a sandwich?'

'Something light?' said Baldwin. 'Wheelers then,' he said to the driver. 'Not the Caprice, Wheelers.'

Judith stared out of the window.

'How's Bertie?' asked Baldwin.

'All right,' said Judith. 'He won't come out when it's raining so I had to leave him behind. Are you doing this because you like seeing me embarrassed? Does it amuse you to put me into a position which makes any outside observer think I am behaving like a child with the sulks?'

'No no no,' said Baldwin. 'What nasty motives you ascribe to me. Do you always make people account for themselves in this way? Perhaps I just wanted to show you my new suit. Do you like it? Tell me frankly, really, what do you think?'

'It's very nice,' said Judith, without enthusiasm.

'Nice stuff, feel,' he said, holding out his arm. 'Neat, businesslike, not exaggerated, that's what I wanted—but I do think it's quite well cut, don't you? And the hat, what d'you think? Rising young barrister? Or not?'

'Oh, I'm sure you'll rise,' she said.

'Of course I shall,' he said. 'Here we are now. My secretary booked a table.'

'But you didn't know you were coming here,' said Judith.

'Hush!' he said.

There was no table, so they sat at the counter and he offered her oysters.

'Yes please,' said Judith.

'You know, I quite thought you were going to refuse to eat,' he said. 'One potted shrimp and a piece of toast melba—that's what I was afraid of.'

'I was going to,' said Judith. 'But then I thought I might as well make it expensive for you.'

'Good, good, good,' he laughed. 'That's what I like to see. What about some really expensive champagne?'

'I suppose so,' she said.

He ordered it. 'We must celebrate,' he said.

'Why?' said Judith.

He laughed again. 'Because, as you say, the whole thing's

unprecedented. And then, apart from anything else, I am genuinely interested in the publishing business. Tell me about it—I'm completely ignorant. Is there money in it these days? How do you get along as a small firm? Do you have big overheads, is it a risky business? You've been going quite a short time, haven't you?'

She answered at some length. After all, she could hardly sit in silence, and it seemed a safe subject. His comments were intelligent and surprisingly brief—she had thought he would have liked talking better than listening. She found herself interested. Publishing had, especially since Anthony's death, absorbed a good deal of her thought and attention.

He seemed to know most of the books they had published, asked her about their authors, then about agents, and foreign publishing, and films, and books in general, turning out to be well-read and discriminating. Then, when the conversation and the champagne had driven away a little of her furious distrust, he began to make suggestions—ideas that might just catch the tide of fashion and become bestsellers, if someone could be found to write them up, distinguished people whose memoirs might be obtainable, people he knew who might be useful. Then, before she could think he was being too interfering, he asked her advice about his own idea for a thriller, to be based on his experience in the Army in Berlin just after the war, told her the whole plot and aroused her interest to such an extent that she could hardly have prevented herself from offering suggestions.

Only as they left the restaurant did she remind herself that this was the man who was blackmailing her because he knew that her dead husband had been a coward. The fact that she had momentarily failed to behave as if she were conscious of this made her now feel that she had been in some way worsted.

She stood in silence on the pavement while they waited for a taxi, wondering how she could get rid of him for the future, how she could in some way undermine his self-confidence, and make sure that he left her feeling that she, not he, had the upper hand.

She was so absorbed that she failed to notice that one of the passers-by had stopped to greet Baldwin, and when the latter said to her: 'Do you know Thomas Hood?' she thought at first he was talking about the nineteenth century poet, and was going to reply that she had read very little by him, when she saw a thin, brown-haired boy holding out his hand to her. She took it and smiled vaguely.

'How d'you do,' said Thomas Hood, politely.

A taxi drew up and he raised his hat to them again as they drove off.

Judith was still wondering what to say to prevent Baldwin from coming to see her again; but partly through failure to find the actual words, she found that they had stopped outside the office before she had spoken at all.

Annoyed, she got out of the taxi without looking at him, and merely saying good-bye without thanking him for the lunch, walked away. When she got back to the office, she was surprised to find that it was already three o'clock.

5

Serena Dryden was coming out next season. The party her parents gave for her early in March was described, oddly, by Lady Dryden, as 'a sort of pre-pre, you know.' In fact, it was not a pre-pre, it was a pre—she had already had a pre-pre—but Lady Dryden was an inexact sort of woman.

Serena's coming-out gave a fillip to the campaign which Lady Dryden had been waging for the last twelve years or more. It gave this indefatigable mother an excuse really to hurl herself again into the fight, in which, since Frances's coming-out four years ago, she had held only ever less powerful weapons. Jane, thank goodness, was married, not brilliantly, but well enough; but there was still Lucinda, still Victoria, still Frances, and now the newest, brightest hope, Serena, whose hair was really golden, not just mousy like the others.

Serena's best friend at school had been Emma Hood—'very

suitable,' her mother said. 'Such charming people and a nice brother and the father dead'—but Emma and her mother being on a visit to some American relations, only Thomas walked his slow way up the wide stairs that evening, greeted his many hostesses with his usual impeccable politeness and settled down by a plate of sandwiches perfectly happy to stand and stare.

The room was crowded; Lady Dryden's parties always were, but there were not a great many people he knew. He talked to one or two of them, had a brief word with Serena, who thought all men impossible until they were forty, and promised several girls whose names he did not know that he would give their love to Emma when he next wrote.

Although his self-possession was often commented upon as being unusual in someone of his age (and it was usually ascribed to the fact that he had been educated largely in France) he had not yet got over a certain difficulty in looking at the faces of people to whom he was talking, less, probably, through doubt as to what he might see in their eyes as through fear of what they might read in his. This, combined with the fact that one of his eyes gave the impression of being less open than the other, made him look a little sly and also rather tired. He had a deep voice, the volume of which he never seemed quite able to control, so that he appeared afraid of making either too much or too little noise. He spoke slowly, but with a great air of earnestness, enunciating his words badly. He was not tall, but lean and healthy-looking.

When he had finished the plate of sandwiches he decided that the prettiest girl in the room was a fair-haired one in scarlet chiffon who was waving a long black cigarette holder and punctuating her conversation with not wholly successful little twirls on one heel. He made his way across to the window in order to examine her from a different angle. Pleased with her left profile, he approached and offered her a cigarette.

'Oh, my dear, how did you know I was panting for another?' she said. 'How terribly sweet of you. Isn't it too awful? I'm trying to give it up but I simply can't. Could you live without it?'

'As a matter of fact, I do,' said Thomas.

'I know, isn't it awful, so do I,' said the girl, standing on one foot, her gaze darting round the room.

'I mean that I don't smoke,' said Thomas.

'You don't smoke?' she said, her huge blue eyes for a moment resting on him. 'Oh, you lucky thing! But you probably drink frightfully. Men always do.'

'Oh, d'you think so?' said Thomas, politely. 'Don't you drink then?'

'Drink? Me?' said the girl, her eyes again like short-sighted searchlights sweeping the sea of faces. 'My dear, I can't stop. Oh, my God, there's Johnny Whitfield, you'll have to stand in front of me. My dear, how too awful. Has he gone?'

'I'm afraid I don't know him,' said Thomas.

'You don't know him?' she said. 'Goodness, how lucky. It's too awful, I can't possibly tell you what happened. Has he gone?'

'I can't tell you because I don't know what he looks like,' said Thomas. 'Has he got a moustache?'

She burst out laughing. 'A moustache? Johnny?' She stood on one leg, clasping the other slim ankle behind her back. 'You *are* funny!'

A pink-faced young man approached, waving both hands behind his ears, and saying in a mock deep voice: 'Ha-ha, who have we here?'

'Johnny *darling*!' cried the girl throwing her arms round his neck. 'I'm never going to speak to you again after you pushed me into that fountain!'

Turning away, Thomas caught sight of Judith Lane. She was standing, talking, in a corner, where he had not noticed her earlier. In black, and with her dark hair pushed away from her face, she looked, this particular evening, beautiful and rather melancholy. She and Anthony had been suitable 'young marrieds' to be asked to Lady Dryden's parties, and somehow Judith had never been crossed off her list.

Thomas went up to her and reminded her that they had met in the street a few days ago, when Baldwin Reeves had introduced them.

'How clever of you to remember,' said Judith.

'You didn't look at me,' said Thomas, in his serious way. 'So how could you remember? But I looked at you.'

'I'm sorry I was so rude,' said Judith.

'I didn't mean that at all,' said Thomas. 'Are you Russian?'

'No,' said Judith.

'Oh,' he said. 'I've never met a Russian woman, but I always imagined somehow they looked like you. But perhaps they don't.'

'I thought they were fat with bobbed hair and greasy faces,' said Judith. 'I don't know whether that's what you meant.'

'No, not that sort so much,' said Thomas. 'I meant the ones who escape on sledges in the middle of the night all wrapped in white furs and chased by wolves.'

'That's much better,' said Judith.

'In *War and Peace*, though, she had a hairy face, d'you remember?' said Thomas.

'Don't you think it was more in the nature of a soft down?' said Judith.

'Do you read Russian novels?' he asked.

'Well, I don't read them, no, really,' she said. 'I have at various times. I had a passion for Turgenev once, I remember.'

'Oh,' he said. 'Are you married?'

'I was, but my husband died.'

'Good Heavens,' he said. 'How awful. What did he die of?'

'He was killed in Korea.'

'I see. How ghastly.' Impressed, he would have liked to have gone on talking about this, but instead he asked her if she thought Baldwin Reeves was clever.

'Quite clever, I think,' said Judith. 'But not at all nice.'

'No, but still . . .' said Thomas. 'So many young people these days seem to have no ambition. I think they ought to have it, don't you? But they seem to think of nothing but being secure and comfortable and out of trouble. I suppose it's the war. Have you got any children?'

'No,' said Judith.

'I don't like children very much,' said Thomas, comfortingly.

'And are you going to be great?' asked Judith.

'I'm supposed to be going into the Diplomatic Service,' said Thomas. 'But I've got to go to Oxford first for three years. It's an awful bore.'

'A bore?'

'Three years,' said Thomas. 'It's such a waste of time. And then the Army. Oh, I'd better get you another drink.' He took her glass, and walked away, then came back to say, 'Don't go away, will you?'

Lucinda Dryden, passing, asked Judith if she would like to be introduced to anybody.

'As a matter of fact,' said Judith, 'I'm in the middle of a conversation with someone simply sweet whose name I don't know. He's very young, and I'm feeling tremendously grown-up.'

'Oh, Thomas Hood,' said Lucinda. 'I saw you talking to him. He is rather nice, isn't he? Mummy thinks he'd do for Serena.'

Judith said: 'Shall I tell him how wonderful Serena is?'

With this in mind, she asked him when he came back whether he had known the Drydens long.

'Serena's a friend of my sister Emma,' he answered. 'They're both coming out this year, but Emma and my mother are in America until next month.'

'Then you I suppose will be coming out too,' said Judith. 'I mean you'll go to dances every night.'

'I'm going to Israel,' said Thomas. 'Have you ever been there? I've got a great friend whose father's a Cabinet Minister there —he's going next month and I want to go with him, if they'll let me—my mother I mean. I want to see it, I'd like to help—well, I mean, how can I really?—but don't you think it's exciting, starting a new country?'

Flushed, he was desperately anxious that she should share his enthusiasm, that she should treat it without the disapproval with which his mother regarded it. To his relief, she seemed to take it quite as a matter of course, and in his excitement he told her everything he knew or had ever thought about Israel, until, seeing her look round the now gradually emptying room, he said: 'I'm afraid I must be boring you. I'm sorry I went on so long.'

'No, I'm very interested. I should say if I wasn't,' said Judith. 'But I think I ought to go soon.'

'Will you have dinner with me?' he asked. 'Oh, no, you're probably doing something.'

She tried to refuse, thinking he was probably asking her simply because he thought he ought to, and also not certain whether he might not become boring after a time, but in the face of his evident disappointment she asked him instead to come back to dinner with her, and went off to telephone Jean-Claude. It was, after all, a diversion: her life lately had been too full of Baldwin Reeves and the apprehensions and memories aroused by him.

'I ought to warn you that the door will be opened by a midget,' she said on the way. 'People are sometimes surprised. It's like that game that always used to reduce me to hysteria as a child—people putting their heads round the door where you don't expect them, coming in on their hands and knees and so on, you know what I mean.'

'Why do you have a midget?' he asked.

'I found him in Paris,' she replied. 'After Anthony died—my husband—my mother-in-law gave me some money to go abroad for a holiday, and she suggested that I should stay with various people, to take my mind off it. So in Paris I stayed with some people I didn't know very well—he was assistant military attaché, and his wife was very pretty and we went to lots of parties and I hated it more and more—oh, well, that's neither here nor there. Jean-Claude was a relation of their cook's, and he was always hanging round, muttering and complaining, which is what he does all the time. One day I got into conversation with him, and it was rather comforting to find someone who hated everybody even more than I did. He told me how he hated the French, they were so mean—he's French himself, of course, and terribly mean—so I offered him a job in England. That's all.'

In spite of her warning, Thomas was taken aback by Jean-Claude's usual ferocious manner.

'Are you sure he's safe?' he asked, when the midget had gone downstairs.

'Oh, he has a heart of gold really,' said Judith. 'At least I suppose he has. I know very little about him, considering we live in the same house. He never goes out or sees anyone. I tried to make him at first, but he says he doesn't want to. I think food's the only thing that interests him—it's the only thing he talks about with any enthusiasm. He has a little stool so that he can reach the stove. I'm terribly fond of him really, but I've no particular reason to suppose he likes me, except that he stays here.'

The dinner was certainly delicious, but Thomas was in that particular respect not the perfect guest he was in almost every other way. Food to him was merely a necessary means of subsistence. The house in general, though, delighted him. He noticed everything, and after dinner, examining her books, asking her about her life, he talked so much she wondered, much as she liked him, whether he would ever go.

'You're getting tired,' he said at last. 'I'll go at once. I'm sorry I've talked so much—I don't usually. I really don't.'

She was sitting on the sofa with Bertie beside her. 'I've loved it, really,' she said.

'Do you go out a lot, what do you do?' he asked. 'No, I ask too many questions, don't I? Do you have lots of lovers, though, being a widow, I mean?'

'Not at the moment, no,' said Judith, smiling.

'You don't mind my asking, do you?' he said. 'I mean, I was just interested. Do you not because you think it's wrong?'

'I don't really want to,' said Judith. 'I suppose I may suddenly feel a tremendous need for a lover one day—in which case it will be time enough to consider the moral problem, don't you think?'

'Could it be me?' he said.

'Who be you?' she asked.

'When you need one, I mean,' he said. 'A lover.'

'Oh,' said Judith. 'Don't you think I should be a bit old for you?'

'No,' he said.

Seeing that she had offended him, Judith said: 'Oh well, I can't say I anticipate its happening in the immediate future—this tremendous need, I mean—so I don't think we need worry for a bit.'

'Oh, that's all right,' said Thomas. 'I don't mind how long it is. I must go now. Would you like me to put Bertie out for you first, then you needn't get cold?'

'That's a wonderful idea,' said Judith, touched. 'Go on, Bertie.'

According to his nightly custom, Bertie rolled over very slowly and lay with his feet in the air and his eyes shut. Thomas picked him up and carried him, hot and heavy, out into the street.

It was not until over a month later that Baldwin Reeves asked Judith for some more money.

He had been into the office several times since she had had lunch with him, and his friendship with Hanescu was advancing rapidly, strengthened by the fact that he had obtained for the latter an invitation to a very promising party. Fisher was impressed by him, Miss Vanderbank thought him awfully attractive. When Judith told Feliks that she had reason to believe he was an unpleasant character and that she herself was particularly anxious never to see him again, Feliks showed little sympathy.

'This is not like you,' he said. 'Do you think I can't look after myself? For Heaven's sake, I'm an unpleasant character myself. Perhaps that's why I like Mr. Reeves. If you don't like him, you needn't see him. But he can be useful to us you know—he's got a lot of contacts.'

Judith had resigned herself to hearing from time to time that cheerful voice in Feliks's room, and to passing him occasionally in the outer office. Fortunately his interest in her seemed to have waned; he confined himself to a polite greeting. She kept

The Times Literary Supplement and the *Bookseller* for reading in the lavatory on the days when he arrived.

She saw Thomas Hood once or twice. He brought his friend David Weitzmann to dinner, a bright-eyed witty boy, the violence of whose opinions about everything she found rather tiring. Thomas's gentler enthusiasms and smaller problems seemed to her much more sympathetic than this boy's sophisticated definiteness; in fact she found herself enjoying the slightly unusual relationship she had with him. Sometimes she felt patronising, often flattered, sometimes he made her feel nostalgic for a time which she had in fact not enjoyed, a time when life had seemed so important and so unfair, when one had worried about one's soul. There were not, after all, so many years between them, but he was at so different a stage that she sometimes felt there were far more. He was simpler than she had been, and more impatient; yet he could on occasions, just as she was on the point of an indulgent laugh, make an observation of such ruthless penetration that she felt she had misjudged him. He could be silly, but even that she rather enjoyed.

One evening she sent Jean-Claude to see a French film at the Classic cinema. From time to time she would insist on his going out, and she found that the cinema was the outing he least disliked. Her first thought when in answer to a knock she opened the door and saw Baldwin Reeves was that he must have known Jean-Claude was out. The thought that he might have been watching the house for days was so disturbing that she let him come in and follow her into the drawing-room before she could protest. She finally told herself that it must be a coincidence: but all the same she did not like to ask him.

He was looking pale, and, rather to her relief, did not greet her with the joviality he affected in the office.

'I'm afraid I must ask you for money,' he said without preliminaries.

'Why?' she asked.

'The £500 didn't go far,' he said. 'I had a lot of debts.'

'How much do you want?' she asked.

'I should like £100 now, and another £300 by the end of the month,' he said.

'I refuse to give it to you,' said Judith.

'Right,' he said, apparently unsurprised.

He drew a large unsealed envelope out of his pocket. 'I shall post this as soon as I leave this house.' He put it back in his pocket and picked up his hat.

'I should like to see it please,' said Judith.

'Certainly.' He handed her the envelope. 'Incidentally, I have plenty of other copies.'

She pulled a thick document out of the envelope. Some newspaper cuttings and photographs fell to the floor. She saw a faded picture of Anthony wearing battle dress, leaning against a tank and laughing. She felt sick. Unrolling the document she found a covering letter to James Blow of the *Sunday News*. She skimmed through it. 'Sensational *exposé* . . . name surely not forgotten . . . built up as a hero . . . the scandalous war . . . discomfiture of many people in high places . . . my own reluctance . . . public should know . . . fully documented.' The next page was headed 'Anthony Lane—Hero or Coward?' and several pages of typescript followed.

She handed the envelope back to him.

'I completely fail to understand how you can write anything so appalling,' she said.

'Yes, it's nasty isn't it?' he said. 'I shall try to keep my own name out of it if possible, but I may not be able to.'

She found that he had, quite gently, pushed her back into a chair and given her a cigarette. She looked at him as he lit it.

'You behave so fantastically,' she said. 'That it's quite impossible for me to know what to do. I should like now to have hysterics and throw things at you, but you're so calm, so unlike what you really must be, that I can't do anything. I'm simply bemused.'

'I'll explain myself. It's quite simple.' He had bent down to light her cigarette and now stayed crouching in front of her, talking quickly and rather breathlessly, 'I'm conceited. Rightly or wrongly, I believe myself to be exceptionally talented. All right, I haven't done much so far. I'm thirty-one. I spent nine years in the Army because in 1946 when I signed on for another seven years I was twenty-one and I hadn't a penny. My parents were dead, I had no idea what had happened to my brother. I couldn't afford to qualify myself for a career. So I stayed in the Army and read for the Bar. Now I'm a barrister and doing all right. I'm known to be clever, I'm beginning to be heard of, in another year or two I shall begin to earn some money. I've had articles in weekly papers that get noticed, I know a lot of people, I've fought one election and by the time I've enough money I shall be in Parliament. Already there are people who think of me as a hopeful young Tory. I make speeches, I talk, I write—it doesn't get reported much yet, you wouldn't have heard about it—but it's all building up to something. You see?'

He was now sitting on the floor looking up at her as if with the greatest anxiety that she should understand him.

'Now, I've got to have money. Not a great deal, but some. Without money I can do nothing, I can get nowhere. You might as well be dead as be poor. I'm making a bit, I shall make more. I manage, just, but I need more. You've got some, I know, because of the Lanes. The Lanes are still very rich—I found that out. I know that even apart from whatever Anthony left you you can always fall back on them. I have a means of making you give me some of that money. Frankly, I don't want to publish that stuff about Anthony. I liked him. I hated him, and envied him, but at the same time I liked him—one did. But I shall publish it. Don't make any mistake about that. I shall send this envelope off tonight, unless you give me the money.'

He stood up, and began to walk about the room.

'All right, you say it's a filthy thing to do. It's blackmail. It's wicked. I shall go to Hell. But I don't believe in Hell. Or Heaven. I'm not a Christian at all. I don't believe in immortality. I don't believe in anything. Except myself. So why should I conform to the Christian ethic? I believe it's all here on earth, in one life, and that we are what we make ourselves. So I want to make myself something big, something powerful. For that I want, at the moment, money. To get money, the easiest way at the moment—apart from working for it, which I do as well—is to blackmail you.'

He stood looking at her as she sat hunched in her chair, then he turned away and began to walk up and down again.

'At first I rather enjoyed it. I hadn't known at all what it was going to be like, and I found myself enjoying it. Now I don't enjoy it so much, partly I suppose because the novelty's worn off, partly because I like you much better than I thought I was going to. Also I had anticipated having you much more in my power, and that I should have enjoyed.'

After a pause, Judith asked: 'What was your object in coming to my office, making me have lunch with you, making friends with Feliks. Was that all power politics too?'

'Partly,' he answered. 'Partly I wanted to talk to you. You say how can I take someone I am blackmailing out to lunch. I say why not? I don't know many women like you; I find them frightening, and the small hold I have over you means I needn't be so afraid.' He sat down opposite her. 'So you see the whole thing is perfectly simple.'

'And when you have power?' asked Judith.

He smiled. 'I shall exercise it with as much reason and judgment as I shall by then have acquired.'

'It all sounds very dangerous to me,' said Judith. 'And the result, I should have said, of rather indiscriminate reading.'

She was pleased to see him flush; but all the same there was something impressive about his self-confidence, his energy—she had felt it all the time.

'Nobody ever has enough money,' she said. 'So I presume you will go on blackmailing me for ever.'

'No, no, certainly not,' said Baldwin. 'Only in real necessity.'

'What a comfort,' said Judith. 'Well, I will give you £100 tomorrow if you come here at seven o'clock. I can't give you any more.'

'I must have the other £300 by the end of the month,' said Baldwin.

'I haven't got it,' said Judith.

'Then you'll have to ask the Lanes.'

'That's out of the question.'

He went towards the door. 'I'll be here at seven,' he said.

'You've got to help me, Feliks,' Judith said the next morning. 'You're always saying you're my only friend.'

'My dear, there's nothing I wouldn't do for you.'

It was one of Feliks's mornings for looking literary. Leaning back in his chair, with his feet on his desk, he was dangling an untidy manuscript in one hand and had a pile of several more beside him. He was wearing a tweed suit which was rather too big for him, a big floppy bow tie, suede shoes, and a pair of very large horn-rimmed glasses which Judith had never seen before. He was smoking, with apparent distaste, a pipe.

'I don't know about that,' said Judith. 'I asked you to stop seeing Baldwin Reeves and you paid no attention at all.'

'Ah, but that was for your own good,' said Feliks. 'Obviously I can't do anything that would jeopardise our mutual business interests.'

'Whatever the reason?' asked Judith.

Feliks took his feet off the desk. 'All right, tell me,' he said.

'He's blackmailing me,' said Judith.

'Oh, don't be absurd,' said Feliks. 'I never heard anything so ridiculous. My poor darling, what can you conceivably have done to be blackmailed about?'

'It's nothing to do with what *I've* done,' said Judith.

After a moment's thought, Feliks said: 'Anthony?'

Judith nodded.

'Good Lord,' said Feliks. 'I suppose he was queer.'

'No, of course not,' said Judith. 'Besides, how could anyone blackmail me if he had been? No, I can't tell you what it was, but it was something some people might be quite interested to know, and which his family would be horrified either to be told themselves or to let other people know.'

'Tell the police,' said Feliks.

'I can't,' said Judith. 'All he's got to do is post the story off to a newspaper. He's got it all ready.'

'It's really news, is it?' said Feliks. 'The police might stop it being published.'

'I don't think they'd have any right to,' said Judith. 'And if they did, you know what journalists are—they'd have seen the story—it would get about. Someone would be bound to print it one day. What's to stop them?'

'I suppose you're right,' said Feliks. 'They made such a fuss about him, of course. He really was a hero. It's extraordinary how people still remember—there was a story about him only the other day in some paper I read. And I suppose he really wasn't a hero at all?'

'Something like that,' said Judith.

'I never really saw him in the part of course,' said Feliks. 'Well, well, well. . . .'

'Don't just sit there and grin,' said Judith. 'What am I going to do?'

'God knows,' said Feliks. 'You'll have to pay him, I suppose, if you don't want the story to get out.'

'Of course I don't,' said Judith. 'Surely I ought to defend his reputation if I can? And besides, his mother would probably die.' She paused. 'I thought perhaps—if you talked to him, without of course letting him know I've told you, but just asking him to leave me alone. I mean he might pay more attention to you, being a man—and he says he wouldn't do it unless he was so poor—I mean he's not completely brutal—I suppose.'

Feliks frowned. 'Is there any point in my making an enemy of him?' he said. 'We mustn't underestimate him, you know. He knows a great many people. He could do me a lot of harm.'

'Oh, but. . . .' Judith started, then stopped. 'Then you can't think of anything?' she said.

Feliks looked embarrassed. 'My dear, I can't honestly say I can. I'll think about it. I really will.'

Judith went back to her room, sat down and cried.

Before long Feliks burst in. 'I've had a brilliant idea,' he said. 'Jimmy Chandos-Wright!'

'What about him?' said Judith.

Jimmy Chandos-Wright was a rich retired criminal whose memoirs they had recently published.

'Have him bumped off,' said Feliks, delighted with himself.

'Oh,' said Judith. 'D'you think so?'

'Of course,' said Feliks. 'Jimmy's boys would do a job like this as easy as kiss your hand. I'll ring him up.'

'Well, but someone might find out,' said Judith.

'Are you kidding?' said Feliks. 'They've done hundreds of these jobs. They don't get nabbed.'

He hurried out of the room, leaving Judith dazed at her desk, and came back a few minutes later to say he had arranged for Jimmy Chandos-Wright to come into the office next week.

'There, you see,' he said triumphantly. 'The whole problem solved.'

'Yes, but I don't know that really . . .' Judith began, doubtfully.

'Talk it all over with him, that's all,' said Feliks. 'You're committed to nothing.'

Halfway out of the room he turned back and, putting a hand on her shoulder, said, 'Don't worry. You know there's nothing I wouldn't do for you, don't you?' He kissed her on the forehead.

'Yes,' she said. 'I know.'

6

It was Spring, even at Harris. Even at Harris, there were buds and lambs and nesting birds. Even at Harris, the air softened and patches of sunlight scurried in front of the huge cloud shadows across the moors.

The gardens of the other, burnt, house were famous for their daffodils. They grew all round the edges of what had once been the lawn; even the shrubbery was now full of them; they were all over the woods and the lake reflected thousands of them. Later on there would be a carpet of lilies of the valley, and of course there were the rhododendrons. That was what had happened when the place was abandoned.

Nanny had read that it was going to be a bad summer. Every time the sun, a little doubtfully, came out, every time a window was opened or Mrs. Lane went out without her gloves, Nanny said: 'They say this is the only mild weather we shall get this year. They say it's going to be the coldest summer on record, and the wettest. Terrible, isn't it, how the weather's been lately. They say it's nothing to do with the atom bomb experiments, but I wonder. I just wonder, that's all. They wouldn't like it to get about that it was, would they? Naturally they say it's nothing to do with the atom bomb. Naturally. But I just wonder.'

Mrs. Lane gardened, and drove to committees on this and that in her powerful car—she was a Rural District Councillor. She was making, very slowly and with exquisite care, a new set of chair seats in *petit point* for the dining-room, and in the evenings she would sit sewing for hours, in silence. No one knew what, if anything she was thinking.

Sir Ralph, encouraged by the milder weather to loiter too long in the garden, had a bad attack of lumbago, and gave vent to his annoyance in a ferocious letter to his bank manager.

'I've really caught him out this time,' he said to Judith. 'Fellow can't add. Or else he's trying to swindle me. What's the use of a bank manager who can't add?'

'But d'you suppose he does his own adding?' asked Judith gently.

'Of course he does,' said Sir Ralph. 'What's he for if he doesn't? He's not the Governor of the Bank of England. Of course he does his own adding. Trying to cheat me, that's what it is. He's completely left out a cheque for £50 I paid in last week. Ha. Thinks I'm too silly to notice I suppose. I've written him a snorter, a real snorter. Dignified, but a snorter. Teach him his place.'

He was sitting at his desk in the library, with four large ledgers beside him and two more open in front of him. The reason for this quantity was partly his complicated system of checking and counter-checking, and partly because he believed that it was much safer to have two or three accounts at the Bank rather than only one—in some obscure way he felt that it fooled the bank manager.

'Well, of course, it's all a great problem, isn't it, money. . . .' Judith said, looking out of the window.

'Money?' said Sir Ralph. 'One of the most interesting things in the world. And sex, I suppose, and possibly politics. Talking about politics, how's your friend Ramsay Macdonald Jones?'

'He really is a problem,' said Judith. 'Baldwin Reeves.'

'Told you the story about Ramsay Macdonald didn't I?' said Sir Ralph.

'Yes you did,' said Judith.

'Oh. Pity. Problem is he?' said Sir Ralph. 'Making a nuisance of himself?'

'Yes,' said Judith. 'In a way.'

'In the prison camp with Anthony was he?' said Sir Ralph. 'They made them get up early I imagine, there.'

'Get up early?' said Judith. 'I suppose so.'

'Don't suppose they gave them a very good breakfast either,' said Sir Ralph. 'What? Some sort of porridge or something, was it?'

'I don't know,' said Judith. 'I didn't ask.'

'Oh,' said Sir Ralph. 'Like to check that addition for me?' He handed her a sheet of paper. 'She takes away the nibs you know. Still, this is a neat page, a neat month April.'

'It looks all right to me,' said Judith, giving him back his calculations.

'I don't often make a mistake,' said Sir Ralph. 'Anthony not behave well?'

'No,' said Judith.

'I knew him very well, you know,' said Sir Ralph. 'Don't think I didn't. Had no father, of course, poor boy. H'm. Better not tell his mother. Wouldn't like it.'

'No, I won't,' said Judith.

'The trouble is,' said Sir Ralph. 'The trouble is I can't get him to send my statement in on the last day of the month instead of the first day of the next month. I like to keep the whole thing up to date to the day, you see.'

There was silence. Getting to her feet, Judith walked slowly over to the window and stood staring out, waiting.

After perhaps as much as ten minutes, Sir Ralph said: 'I wonder if I could get him to send me fortnightly statements? Might keep him up to the mark a bit.'

After another long pause, Judith said: 'He wants money.'

'Of course he does,' said Sir Ralph. 'That's why he cheats me. But he's got his salary, hasn't he?'

'I meant Baldwin Reeves,' said Judith.

'Oh him,' said Sir Ralph. 'Fatuous name.' He added: 'Money? Why?'

'So that no one shall know about Anthony.'

Sir Ralph frowned. 'Sounds a funny sort of fellow.'

'I've given him £600 so far,' said Judith.

'Oh, no no no,' said Sir Ralph, with sudden emphasis. 'That won't do at all. Can't have that. You must allow me to regard this completely as my affair. I shall reimburse you for what you have already given him and any other demands you must pass straight on to me. Is that understood?'

'But no, I didn't mean that,' said Judith.

'There's no question about it,' said Sir Ralph. 'Why should you pay? It was my blood, my dear, not yours.'

'I don't want the money back, really,' said Judith, tearfully.

'I've got a new cash book here, a perfectly good one,' said Sir Ralph. 'I shall keep a record of the whole business. Now does this bring you up to date?'

'Well, yes, I think so,' said Judith.

'If he asks for more, let me know at once,' said Sir Ralph, writing busily. 'He'll wonder what all this is about, I daresay.'

'The bank manager will, you mean?' said Judith.

'Of course he will,' said Sir Ralph.

'You can't think of any way out of it, I suppose?' said Judith. 'I have tried to, but I don't see what else we can do.'

'You don't know his mother as I do,' said Sir Ralph. 'You don't, you know. Bad for the Government too. Bad all round.

Bad for morale. Besides, you know, disgrace is disgrace, what-ever the modern idea may be. We have to defend his honour, for all he didn't himself. Sorry for you, my dear—unpleasant business. Sounds a nasty fellow, Reeves.'

'I'm so glad I told you,' said Judith.

'We'll deal with it,' said Sir Ralph. 'I'll keep an exact record—that's the best thing, I think. He'll wonder, I daresay. Still you've got to keep a check on them—that'll keep him on his toes.' He reached for his cheque book. Judith was not quite certain whether he was talking about his bank manager or his blackmailer.

The dying Othello clawed the curtains of Desdemona's white and crimson bed. His black hand reached her golden hair, his tortured face bore down upon her white serene one; the watchers in the shadows stood motionless; sobbing and singing Othello died, and the curtain fell.

The applause broke, and swelled. The huge cast bowed, and bowed again; then the soloists appeared, Iago, then Desde-mona, then Othello.

'They'll get Kubelik up in a minute,' the man next to Baldwin Reeves said, stamping his feet. And there sure enough he was and the man beside Baldwin cried 'Bravo! Bravo!'

Acclaiming again the two principals who, splendidly dressed and grandly smiling, kept up the illusion of being altogether larger than life, Baldwin's eyes filled with tears. The opera it-self had been wonderfully moving; for a moment he found the culminating applause almost more so.

On the way out he saw several people he knew, to most of whom he had already spoken in the intervals since he was not a man to hold back once he had seen an acquaintance. He was alone, but wearing a dinner jacket, which made them think, if they thought at all, that he was going on somewhere. This was of course the impression he had intended to give. In fact he took a bus to Parliament Square, and walked along Victoria Street to his flat near Westminster Cathedral.

He was an intelligent man. Judith in her few conversations

with him had already discovered this rare quality in him; and because she was something of an intellectual snob it had annoyed her. She would rather not have found her enemy possessed of the quality she most admired.

His behaviour for all that was often far from rational. For instance, his going to Covent Garden in a dinner jacket so that people might not know that his whole evening was in fact to be spent alone was nothing like as petty as some of the ruses to which he would resort in order to impress, or frighten, or otherwise impose himself upon even the least important people. He was unable, or at all events unwilling, to compete on equal terms: he had to be either above or below his rivals. His 'rivals' were of course everyone else in the world. Being below them involved various subterfuges, such as pretending to be completely unable to do certain things which he in fact could do, but badly. For instance, he found certain practical accomplishments, such as driving a car or mending an electric light fuse, extremely difficult. He would therefore make great play with the idea that he found them impossible, and would exaggerate his inefficiency with an appealing air of hopelessness. The same applied to his few social failures. There were one or two people whom he completely failed to charm. Realising this, he would be very rude to them, and then in the same self-deprecating way would tell everyone what had happened, exaggerating both his rudeness and the other person's dislike of him—which had the effect of making him seem disarmingly modest and able to laugh at himself, and of taking the sting out of anything the other person might say about him, he having as it were got it in first.

All these little manœuvres had been part of his life since his earliest youth. He had been an exceptionally clever little boy. At his grammar school he had been for some time the youngest as well as the poorest boy—his father was a respectable village chemist, but everyone knew that his mother was an invalid and that they had no money at all. Not content with his reputation for brightness, Baldwin had built it up into one of brilliance by concealing the fact that he ever did any work. He would ostentatiously read novels during 'prep.' periods, and play with a white mouse or draw caricatures of the masters in class, so that when he passed all his examinations with distinction his glory was greatly enhanced by the fact that he was known to have done no work at all. In fact, of course, he had worked at home during the night.

Apart from his conceit, Baldwin Reeves had been quite a normal, high-spirited schoolboy, save only in one particular. He very seldom spoke. For one thing, he was overwhelmingly shy. For another, when he was eleven, a boy, rather older than himself, who had been his greatest friend and to whom he had been selflessly devoted, found grander friends and turned against Baldwin, even inciting some of his new friends to bully him. This made Baldwin for some years very bitter against humanity. Then his home life was not happy, his mother being constantly ill and his father's spirit having been quite broken by this misfortune. Also, in spite of his disillusion, he was an emotional boy, and being too young to understand in the least any of his feelings, he was made tongue-tied by them.

However it may have been, his silence, particularly in conjunction with his cleverness, was considered by his masters to be extraordinarily sinister. His perfectly normal naughtiness was made by them into something much more wicked, simply because when they spoke to him about it he would turn completely blank, and none of them ever succeeded in getting a response out of him. This attitude had, of course, its effect on him, and he left school with a definite and flattering conviction that he was damned.

The Army made the great change in him. Sent, by the fortunes of war, into a smart regiment, he learnt quickly—among other things, how to be a gentleman. Again he did well, and again he pretended not to try. There, too, he overcame his shyness, and adopted the habitual jollity which was now second nature to him. He learned to speak better English, and became much more adept at dealing with his fellow men. But he still kept his distance. His women friends were always stupider than he was, and usually common; he had no men friends. He took his Bar exams at an obvious disadvantage, being also in the Army. Pretending to have social engagements which were in fact non-existent was so much a part of his life that he often did it without reason, even half deceiving himself. His ambition was huge, but everything was to be achieved as it were at an angle, not in a straight line.

Lately, for the first time, the points system on which he conducted his relations with other people had been beginning to show its failings. He was now meeting a number of other intelligent people, and the unusual and far from intimate nature of his relations with them made it difficult for him to learn as much from them as he would have liked to. He was quite conscious of this, but did not know what to do about it. In an odd sort of way, it made him insist even more on being always a little different: slightly puzzled, he clung more tenaciously to each little hold he had over anyone.

All this was reflected in his attitude to Judith, over whom he really did have a hold, a hold so strong that, oddly enough, he already found himself being more frank in conversation with her than with anyone else. The fact that he was beginning to doubt whether he really was so different, or at least so damned, made him rejoice in the undoubted unconventionality—to put it at its mildest—of his behaviour to her. For if he was not different and damned then what was he? His self-confidence, though it seemed so vast, was not really strong enough to face a fight on equal terms. Also he was by now attracted to Judith, but here he made a mistake—he thought it was the relationship which attracted him.

The morning after he had been to Verdi's Othello, he rang up Miss Vanderbank and asked her to have lunch with him. There were several things about both Judith and the firm of Hanescu Lane which he thought it might be extremely useful for him to know, and Miss Vanderbank had seemed a co-operative source of information.

She, delighted, thanked Goodness she had brought her hat that morning, and tripped happily off to meet him.

She was so easily impressed that he found himself enjoying her company. They had an amusing lunch; he was rather flirtatious and she bridled gaily at each sally. She told him, unintentionally, almost all she knew about Judith, and about the firm.

Miss Vanderbank's only blind spot was Feliks. In spite of everything, including his evident indifference, she loved him. She always had. So when Baldwin asked her about the relations between Judith and Feliks she emphatically, and with a pang of useless jealousy, denied that there was anything between them. Then, as she sometimes did, she became rather sentimental about Judith.

'There she is,' she said. 'So young and everything. And he was so good-looking, the husband, he really was. It's a tragedy really, isn't it? If only she could find a nice husband.' Miss Vanderbank sighed. She had often said the same thing to Fisher in the office, and almost brought tears to the eyes of that sympathetic youth. 'She's so sweet. I'm sure anybody would like to marry her. But of course, I suppose, if you've once been married to someone like him—I mean, he was a hero wasn't he? —it isn't easy to accept a second best. She turns them all away, you know, and Mr. Hanescu's always saying to her she should go out more, but she just sits at home with her little dog and that midget servant. I really believe they're the only creatures she cares for in the world.'

'Why the midget?' asked Baldwin. 'I thought he was a most unpleasant creature.'

'Oh, she's fond of him, I don't know why,' said Miss Vanderbank. 'She brought him back from Paris with her once, soon after her husband died, and he's been with her ever since. I think he's very devoted to her and that makes her fond of him, you know.'

'Too fond?' asked Baldwin.

'Don't be ridiculous,' said Miss Vanderbank with spirit.

'Sorry,' said Baldwin, embarrassed. 'I just wondered.'

Feeling that he had lost her sympathy, he changed the subject, unable all the same to forget the annoyance that what she had said had caused him. 'What business has she to be devoted to a dwarf?' he thought later, in the bus going back to his Chambers.

The thought of the disrespectful little creature lurked in his mind all day. He worked late, and going back tired to his gloomy flat he gazed at himself in the mirror, seeing a slightly dirty face with eyes staring to try to frighten himself, and said: 'The dwarf must go.'

When Judith went to the office the next day, she found Fisher uneasily lounging about in her room.

He had a Christian name—it was Henry—but, in so far as he was known at all, he was known as Fisher. He was a long thin greenish young man, very polite and sad: he often sent people flowers, especially Miss Vanderbank, who was one of the chief causes of his sadness. He was also worried about his career, because he wanted very much to be a successful literary man. At Cambridge he had known happiness, even a modest glory, for he had quite a considerable talent for play production, and had put on a series of dramas by Betti, Pirandello, Brecht and himself, which had attracted some notice; but when he came to London all that was brought to an end by his fearsome widowed mother who, suspecting the influence on her boy of all those nasty acting people had pronounced publishing more suitable, a decision in which she felt strengthened when she saw the nice healthy normal girl with whom he was to share an office.

In the evenings he wrote verse dramas, but since he never attempted a subject less immense than the whole human situation, he found the work very difficult and disheartening. Sometimes he read passages from his plays aloud to a small group of his Cambridge friends, but unfortunately they were a clever lot, who only tolerated him because they hoped one day to have their own works published by Hanescu Lane, and he gained little encouragement from them.

He had inherited from his father, an unromantic but effi-cient business man, some sixty thousand pounds, and none of his money sense. A good deal of what was left from his kind and cultural extravagances at Cambridge was invested in Hanescu Lane & Co.

At the moment it was Miss Vanderbank again.

'She's too generous,' he said to Judith, loping about on the pale grey carpet. 'Really too generous. It makes her do things, you know, which she thinks she's too wise to do. But she's not at all—too wise, I mean. This man Reeves, for instance—I don't think she ought to take up with him, I really don't.'

'Has she been too generous to him?' asked Judith, very coldly.

Fisher blushed. 'She had lunch with him,' he said.

'Yes?' said Judith.

'Yesterday,' said Fisher, as if that made it worse.

Miss Vanderbank happening at that moment to come in with some letters, Judith said to her, casually: 'I hear you've been seeing our friend Reeves.'

'Oh! . . .' Fisher, betrayed, turned his back.

'Oh yes,' Miss Vanderbank said, blithely. 'He gave me lunch.'

'Was he nice?' asked Judith, looking through her letters. 'Amusing?'

'Oh yes,' said Miss Vanderbank. 'We talked about all sorts of things—he's so interesting, isn't he? But . . .' seeing her opportunity, 'Mainly you.'

'Me?' said Judith.

'Oh, he wanted to know everything about you,' said Miss Vanderbank, happily. 'On and on and on. Said he was too shy to ask you himself. I think that sort of man often is shy, don't you? In spite of that confident manner. Sensitive really.'

'Did he say . . . ?' asked Judith. 'What did he say—about me, I mean.'

'Well, he didn't so much say anything,' said Miss Vanderbank. 'Just sort of implied.'

'Implied?' said Judith.

'Well, yes, implied,' said Miss Vanderbank.

'How very odd,' said Judith.

'Well, I must say, I wondered, when he asked me out to

lunch,' said Miss Vanderbank. 'But that's what it was, to ask about you.'

Feliks was shouting in the outer office. 'Where is everyone? Jimmy's here, Judith. In my room.'

'Coming,' called Judith. She smiled at Fisher, who was looking a little shame-faced, and went out of the room, disturbed by Miss Vanderbank's revelations.

When Jimmy Chandos-Wright had been in business, he had had no time for showing off. He had been a largish man in a rather shapeless suit, hard-working, conscientious, and an expert at his job. Only since his retirement had he taken to wearing astrakhan collars and talking as he thought a gangster should.

Most of his life had been spent in burglary. Starting young, he had worked his way to the top. He had imagination, an excellent talent for organisation, and the control over both himself and those who worked for him which is essential in a good crook. There was a time when if you wanted a big job done, anywhere in the world, you asked Jimmy Chandos-Wright (né Green) to do it. He had a reputation for reliability seldom equalled in his particular metier. The police knew all about him, of course, because his work was usually unmistakeable; in fact, the morning after most of his coups, not only the police of the world but all the other burglars, blackmailers, dog-dopers, con-men or what you will, opening their newspapers said: 'That's Jimmy.' He was never caught, not in his heyday—there had been times, before he was really experienced, when he had had a spell or two 'inside'—but in his heyday they couldn't touch him.

Nobody knew what he had done in the war: he himself was uncharacteristically shifty about it, but he had certainly made money. Afterwards he did very well on the Black Market, and fixed one or two big deals in scrap which brought him in a nice sum. He lived in Tangier for a time and undertook a variety of commissions for people who were prepared to pay enormously for him to arrange some irregularity or other.

At last, his fortune made and Lucille, his red-haired girl,

having always had a leaning towards respectability, they married and went to live in Eastbourne. They bought a yacht and spent a considerable part of the year in Cannes, but the only risk Jimmy took these days was at the tables, where as a matter of fact he had exceptional luck.

Several publishers had tried, without success, to persuade him to write his memoirs, but Hanescu's approach had been sartorial. He had introduced him to his tailor, who made something in wide chalk stripes, much collared and cuffed, which delighted Jimmy, and to his shirt-maker, who produced a succession of silk initialled shirts and a masterpiece in horizontal green stripes. It was probably the offer of an introduction to his boot-maker (he had not in fact got one) which finally won Jimmy for Hanescu.

The friendship thus auspiciously begun had thrived, and when the jolly forty-ish Lucille produced the son who was now his parents' pride and joy, the boy was christened Feliks, and Hanescu, together with a rich Jewish bank-breaker, was a god-father.

'Sandy's your boy,' Jimmy said, when Hanescu asked his advice for Judith. 'Sandy'll do you fine. He's a nice boy and doesn't make mistakes.'

He was wearing a black and white check suit and a yellow waistcoat. 'How beastly you look,' Feliks had said when he came in. 'That's not Denton—he'd rather die.'

'Little fellow in Shepherd's Market—very expensive,' said Jimmy. 'King of Spain recommended me.'

'The King of Spain?' said Feliks.

'That's who he said he was,' said Jimmy.

Feliks had explained that Judith might find it necessary to dispose of somebody. Jimmy, unsurprised, praised the talents and discretion of his friend Sandy.

'He's in dog-doping,' he said. 'But he's not happy there. There's money in it of course, but no scope. He was in Tangier with me, one of my best boys. But it got a bit hot and he came back to something quiet and steady for a time. You'll like him, and he'll be glad of a chance to get out of the rut. He's reliable too—I doubt if there's a better man in Europe for what you want, certainly not in England. I'll give him a ring.' He stretched one large hand towards Feliks's white telephone.

'Oh, but. . . .' said Judith.

'Worried about the price?' asked Jimmy, benignly. 'There isn't a man in London could get better terms for you than I can. What d'you want to pay?'

'I don't really know what the usual thing is,' said Judith.

'He'll probably want a grand,' said Jimmy. 'Of course he's a good man. I know fellows who'd do it for a monkey at the drop of a hat, but then you'd be taking more of a risk. Sandy's a real expert. I'll get it done for less than his usual fee, that I can promise you.'

'The only thing is,' said Judith desperately, 'I'm not quite sure yet whether it will be necessary.'

'All right,' said Jimmy. 'You let me know when you're ready and I'll tip him off. O.K.?'

'Thank you very much,' said Judith.

'That's right,' said Feliks, patting her shoulder. 'You let Jimmy know. You'll fix it, won't you, Jimmy?'

'Of course, of course, anything for a friend,' said Jimmy. 'Don't you worry, my dear, there's no risk, not with Sandy. Never slipped up yet, Sandy.'

'I knew we could rely on you, Jimmy,' said Feliks.

7

To a certain extent, of course, Judith was a prig. To a certain, quite small, extent, she was still the scrubbed sixteen-year-old who had commanded the school of which she had been head girl with such devoted efficiency.

Even in her 'intellectual' days, that is to say in the years between her leaving school and her marriage, she had never quite lost that way of looking at things. For instance, though the code she then adopted involved tolerance and even admiration for any sort of unconventional behaviour among her friends, she herself had never really lost her head girl's healthy opinion that 'sex was silly'. This had lasted even beyond her marriage, the principle being only slightly modified—that is to say, sex became silly except with one's husband.

Indeed, it was only in the realm of ideas that she was the free spirit she thought herself. Where behaviour was concerned, where life was to be led, her inclination was towards the safe, the conventional, the duty-guided. Her intelligence, which was not as exceptional as she thought it but was perhaps unusual in a woman, and her eagerness to find a duty whose path to follow, had led her into some strange friendships, into, even, a rather strange marriage; but in spite of everything she had had few moral doubts. Right was right and wrong was wrong. She would not have liked to have heard it expressed by that cliché, but though it perhaps debased her attitude, it more or less summed it up.

With it, she was a fatalist. It was perhaps this last, together with an altogether feminine desire for self-immolation, which made her need to devote herself to a duty, for duty breathed life into the inevitability of events, gave them, if not a meaning, at least something to be suffered for.

Her liking for responsibility was one reason for her liking for Jean-Claude. She wanted dependents. She had enjoyed the days when her widowed father had relied on her; she would have liked to have had a lot of children; in long daydreams she gave herself a kingdom and ruled it with scrupulous fairness and devotion. Jean-Claude was solitary and helpless. He needed to be fed, kept warm, and allowed to cook and clean; that was all he wanted, and Judith, in providing it, gladly assumed him as one of her duties.

When, therefore, Baldwin Reeves after four days of brooding arrived at her house in a self-made rage and ordered her to dismiss Jean-Claude, she was deeply upset. She would rather have paid any money in the world, and said so.

During the last few days, the midget had assumed a disproportionate importance in Baldwin's eyes. The latter's reasoning, being now influenced by various emotions not clear even to himself, was not particularly valid, but it ran, roughly, along these lines. He had found out that to get money from Judith was not hard, but his success had not had what now seemed to be the desired effect on her, for instead of fearing him and acknowledging his power, it was quite obvious that she not only disliked but despised him. She had thawed briefly during one lunch, but had quickly reverted to her usual icy evidence of distaste. He had expected his power to extend to all sorts of aspects of her life: it remained purely financial. This midget had aroused an irritating and unnecessary liking on her part. To force her to get rid of him would show her how much he, Baldwin Reeves, was to be feared, and would at the same time remove the object of, and therefore soon the existence of, this annoying affection.

'I'm sorry,' he said. 'I'm afraid I must insist.'

She had turned pale. When he had told her why he had come there had been a pause, and then, quite suddenly, her face had gone white, and he had thought for a moment that she might faint. It had not occurred to him to change his mind, partly because he felt for some reason as though he had no control now, the whole business simply had to be gone through with: he was obeying orders, even though they were his own.

'Are you not going to give me any reason?' she asked.

'I can't,' said Baldwin.

'But what can anyone have against Jean-Claude?' she asked. 'What can he have done?'

'I'm afraid I can't tell you any more,' said Baldwin. 'I simply want him to go.'

'But what will he do?'

'There are employment agencies, aren't there?' said Baldwin.

'But who'd want a midget?' asked Judith.

'You did,' said Baldwin.

'That's different,' said Judith. 'Besides, he's so ugly.'

'He could go back to France,' said Baldwin.

'Can I keep him until he gets another job?' she asked.

'I'm afraid he must go tomorrow.'

'Tomorrow?' she said, horrified. 'But where will he go?'

'You can give him some money, can't you?' said Baldwin, who had not thought of all these details.

Judith began to walk up and down the room.

'I've told you I'll give you any money you want,' she said.

'I don't want money,' he said.

'You do,' she said. 'You're always saying how much you need money. Or have you found another source of income?'

'No,' he said.

'Why don't you?' she said. 'Why don't you find some more widows with a little money to help me to keep you? Why should I be the only one? I've no doubt you could find plenty more.'

'I don't want to,' he said. 'I simply want you to get rid of the dwarf. I'm not here to discuss money.'

'I want to discuss money,' said Judith. 'I'll give you £500 in three days' time if you leave Jean-Claude alone—and more later. Which would you rather have, £500 or the sadistic pleasure of seeing a harmless midget suffer?'

'Harmless midget suffer,' said Baldwin.

'What about £1,000?' said Judith.

'No,' said Baldwin.

'Anything,' said Judith. 'The house—anything. . . .'

She was pale and obviously deeply agitated, but he felt in a way she should be crying, throwing herself at his feet—then he hoped she wouldn't.

'I must go,' he said. 'And the dwarf tomorrow.'

'No, wait,' she put her hand on his arm. 'Wait.' Would she hit him, he thought confusedly, or throw herself round his neck, or——? 'Wait, isn't there anything you'd rather have?'

He looked at her without saying anything at all, one hand on the door.

'Isn't there?' she said.

The scene became suddenly meaningless to Baldwin. He could hardly remember what it was all about. He wanted desperately to go.

'No, there's nothing,' he said, turning away. 'Nothing at all,' and he went out of the house.

Left alone, Judith sat down to think, to be calm and reasonable and think of a way out, but the whole situation had become so monstrous that her thoughts floundered on the borders of nightmare: she could see no solution. She worked herself up into a rage against Baldwin, for the first time really considering and facing the horror of his behaviour. The rage abated, and left her tired.

Some hours after Baldwin had left, she went downstairs to find Jean-Claude. He was in his small sitting-room, polishing the silver, which was already gleaming, and listening to the wireless, which was turned so low as to be almost inaudible.

'You can have it louder than that,' said Judith. 'It doesn't disturb me at all.'

'S'all right, s'all right,' said Jean-Claude. 'I don't listen.' He turned the wireless off.

There was a silence, broken only by the click of the clean forks dropping into their places.

'Tomorrow,' said Jean-Claude. 'Fish day.' He wrinkled his broad nose. Although he cooked it beautifully, he always expressed the liveliest distaste for all species of fish. 'And for Bertie skin but no bones.' He grinned, because when he had first come, Judith had had great difficulty in making him believe that fish-bones were bad for dogs. 'Dogs eat bones,' he had obstinately repeated, until Judith had threatened to give Bertie his meals herself, which Jean-Claude had considered quite unsuitable.

'Yes,' said Judith. 'Oh, by the way. . . .'

'Yes?' said Jean-Claude.

'I'm afraid. . . .' Judith said. 'I'm afraid there's some rather bad news. I've got to—that is, things have been going rather badly, you see, and I'm afraid I shall have to—it won't be possible for me to keep you.'

'Keep . . . ?' Jean-Claude had not understood.

'I mean that I shan't be able to afford to go on having you here,' said Judith. 'I only wish I could—I'm very upset about it—it's not that I don't wish you could stay for years, but it just—won't be possible you see.'

There was a long pause while Jean-Claude absorbed this information. At last his evident bewilderment gave way to a broad smile.

'Ah, I know,' he said. 'It's always the same old money, money. I know. But look. I wait, I want nothing, later you get rich, you start to pay me again. I wait.'

'Oh, but you see,' Judith said. 'It's very kind of you, but I shall probably have to move from here, and go somewhere smaller where there's no room for you.'

'No small room?' Jean-Claude looked disbelieving. 'You find somewhere with a small room where I go.'

'Well, I. . . .' said Judith. 'I don't know that I shall be able to.'

'You try,' Jean-Claude said.

'Well, yes, I'll try, of course,' said Judith. 'But I may not be able to.'

'Well, then so bad,' said Jean-Claude, shrugging his shoulders. 'But perhaps yes. And until then I stay here and we don't worry.'

'Well, the thing is,' said Judith. 'I know it must seem odd, and I really wouldn't do it if it weren't absolutely necessary—I mean really it's just as bad for me—only I'm afraid it's absolutely essential for you to leave tomorrow.'

There was another pause, then Jean-Claude said in amazement: *'Demain? Je pars demain?'*

'I'm terribly sorry,' said Judith. 'I really am. You can't imagine how awful it is for me.'

'You want me to go tomorrow?' he asked again.

'I don't want you to go at all,' said Judith. 'I wish to goodness you needn't. But I'm afraid you must.'

Jean-Claude had put down the fork he was polishing. Now, very slowly, he picked it up again and began to rub it with his chamois leather. 'So I go tomorrow,' he said.

'I'm terribly sorry,' said Judith. 'Of course you'll easily get another job—I'll give you references and everything—and we'll find you somewhere to stay of course.'

'I go tomorrow,' said Jean-Claude, nodding slowly.

'I wish I could explain,' said Judith. 'I mean why it's neces-sary—it's not that I want you to go.'

The midget shook his head gently.

'I ask no questions,' he said. 'I am a small man. I ask no questions. I go tomorrow.'

Baldwin Reeves was having lunch in the Inner Temple. Sit-ting next to him was a small, bird-like man called David Saint, whose company Baldwin was generally anxious to cultivate, not so much for its own sake as because of the lordly host of relations by which this otherwise insignificant fellow was winged about.

Today, however, even the relations were not enough to hold Baldwin's attention, which had soon wandered from the com-plicated and boring details of the Company Law case on which David Saint was currently engaged. He was so preoccupied, in fact, that he got up in the middle of one of his neighbour's sen-tences, and it was only on turning back to smile good-bye that he realised what he had done and apologised. 'So sorry, old boy, something on my mind. I'd love to hear the end of that— let's lunch here next week——Must rush now.' He hurried out of the Hall, passing in the door two distinguished counsel, one of whom said to him: 'I liked your case this morning, Reeves.'

Usually, Baldwin would have stopped and accepted this op-portunity of getting into conversation with so powerful a man. Today, however, he simply said: 'Oh, thank you, thank you,' and hurried on.

'Hope it goes well,' the Q.C. called after him, then, turning to his companion said: 'He's working himself too hard, that fellow—looks worn out.'

Collecting a bundle of papers which he had left downstairs, Baldwin hurried out into the Strand, hailed a taxi, and giving the address of Judith's house, added: 'Please hurry.'

He had only three quarters of an hour before he was due back in court. He was not even quite certain what he meant to do, but it seemed enormously important to get to her house, and see the midget. Judith herself of course would be at the office.

He rustled nervously through his sheaf of papers. He had meant to have a look at them in the taxi, so as to have one or two points fresh in his mind for the afternoon, but instead he leaned forward to tap on the glass partition and urge on the driver. It was a very old and rattly taxi, and the driver's large back expressed disapproval of this fever for speed. Swearing, Baldwin jerked back into his seat.

They trundled at last down the King's Road.

'Right here,' shouted Baldwin. 'This is it. Turn right.'

Then, when the taxi was half-way round the corner into the street he suddenly battered furiously on the partition, shouting, 'Stop, stop, stop!'

Grumbling, the driver braked, but his passenger had already leapt out, waving his handful of papers and still shouting.

There on the pavement was Jean-Claude, holding in one hand an enormous suitcase and in the other a very small umbrella. Judith had left for the office that morning saying that she would find somewhere for him to stay for a few nights and that on her return that evening she would take him there in a taxi, but it did not seem to him suitable that she should have to take him across London; he thought it better, seeing too how upset she was about it all, that he should leave quietly while she was away at the office. He had packed all his belongings into his one cumbersome old suitcase and clasping his umbrella in his other hand had stumped off with the intention of catching a bus to Victoria.

When Baldwin Reeves, whom he knew vaguely as someone Judith seemed not to like, suddenly appeared in front of him, waving a bundle of papers and shouting incoherently, Jean-Claude, understanding nothing, put his suitcase down and waited.

'Come on, come on, we'll go back,' said Baldwin. He gesticulated at the taxi-driver. 'Go on to number twelve,' he shouted. Picking up Jean-Claude's suitcase, he said, 'Come on, I'll take this.'

'But no,' said Jean-Claude. 'I go the other way.'

There were already a good many cars parked in the little street, and the taxi-driver was prevented from drawing up in front of number twelve by the old white Mercedes which had just stopped there. He went on a little farther, and then got out to keep an eye on his eccentric fare.

Judith, who had just driven up with Feliks in his Mercedes, ran up the steps into her house without looking up the street to where Jean-Claude and Baldwin were arguing.

'I'm so grateful, Feliks, really,' she was saying. 'You'll find him awfully useful, too, I know you will—he doesn't mind what he does. Jean-Claude!' she called down the stairs. 'You may like him so much that you want him to stay longer than a fortnight.'

Going into the drawing-room she took off her coat and, throwing it on to a chair, turned to find Feliks not with her.

'Feliks?' she called. Receiving no answer, she supposed he must have left something in the car, and went to the telephone. She had been trying to speak to Jimmy Chandos-Wright that morning, and had been told that he would be in at two o'clock.

It was with an unconscious relish in the hopelessness of her situation that she had chosen this particular morning to tell him that she would not need his friend's services. She had known all the time that he would have to be told: anything else was ridiculous—murder was hardly even right or wrong, it was simply out of the question. Before the opportunity had been given to her, she would not have known how clear her reaction would be; but in the event she had found the suggestion simply absurd.

'You what?' Jimmy said, when she had told him. 'You don't want him? Baby, you sure are passing something up there. He's a good boy, Sandy. If it's the security angle that's on your mind. . . .'

'No, no, it's not that,' said Judith. 'I'm so sorry to have bothered you but it turned out to be unnecessary after all. If I had wanted it, of course I wouldn't have thought of asking anyone else.'

'Ah, you'd have been making a mistake if you had you know,' said Jimmy. 'I tipped him off there might be something up. He'll be disappointed.'

'I'm so sorry,' said Judith. 'I'm afraid I must go now—there seems to be someone arriving.'

Jean-Claude, whom bewilderment had made even more guttural than usual, was being noisily persuaded by Baldwin to return to the house; following them came Feliks, asking questions; and in the background, detached but watchful, was the taxi-driver.

'All right, all right, I know,' Baldwin was saying. 'It doesn't matter about the train. Come on, for God's sake. I've got to go.'

'But what are you doing?' said Feliks again. 'What are you doing, Baldwin? Do tell me what you're doing.'

'What are you doing?' Judith asked too, but so angrily that Feliks at once stopped his vague questionings, and Baldwin, his hand still on Jean-Claude's shoulder, looked at her in alarm and without answering.

'What are you doing?' Judith said again. The sight of him made her realise what heights of hate she had reached since last she saw him. She was so angry that she felt her nostrils and her upper lip quivering. This evidence of the strength of her own emotion impressed her and gave her a sense of power.

'My dear. . . .' Feliks, who enjoyed scenes but preferred them to be engineered by, and centred upon, himself, approached her cautiously with one peace-making hand raised.

The intervention broke into Baldwin's stare.

'Well, there he is, there he is,' he pushed the midget forward. 'And the suitcase.' Resuming his air of desperate hurry, he swung the suitcase into the middle of the room, thumped it down and turned to go.

'All right, I want to go back,' he said to the taxi-driver. 'Oh, the umbrella. Here you are,' he held out to Jean-Claude the umbrella which he still held in one hand. The midget drew back. 'No, come on, take it, take it.'

In pressing it into Jean-Claude's hand, Baldwin dropped

several of the papers which he was still clasping. He bent to pick them up.

'Got to be back by half past,' he said.

No one else moved or spoke, Feliks because he understood nothing of what was going on and was annoyed because he felt left out, Jean-Claude because it was safer to do nothing, and Judith because she liked to see Baldwin discomfited.

'Must have these things, blast them,' Baldwin said. 'Need them for this afternoon. Can't you be turning round? Oh, he's gone. Is he turning round? Must be there by half past. All right, I've got them.' He went out of the room without looking round.

'Wait,' Judith suddenly followed him, shutting the door firmly upon the silent figures of Feliks and Jean-Claude. 'What are you doing?'

Taking refuge in violence, Baldwin shouted: 'I've brought him back haven't I? What more d'you want?' Realising that they ought not to be overheard he dropped his voice to a fierce whisper. 'What d'you mean, what am I doing? He's here isn't he, for Christ's sake? I can't spend all day messing about here. I'm supposed to be in court.'

'Why have you brought him back?' said Judith.

His motives were inexplicable even to himself. No one was more surprised than he at what he had done. This made him, of course, unreasonably angry with her. Suddenly seizing her by the shoulders, he went on whispering, furiously: 'You've got him, haven't you? You've got your blasted little midget. Now shut up about it. Take him and shut up. Do whatever you like with him—whatever you do do that makes you so fond of him.'

'I'm not, I don't—what do you mean?' she said.

'Stop asking me what I mean,' he began to shake her, bumping her against the wall. 'I don't mean anything. Now shut up. Take him back and shut up.'

'No, stop it, don't, you're mad,' she put up her hands to try and push him away, upon which he stopped and held her in absolute silence, until she laughed, quite quietly, and said: 'No, but really it is funny.'

'I know,' he said, loosening his clasp on her arms, and beginning to smile, as if he could not help it. 'I know, I know, I know.'

The mood having changed, and needing a remark on which to break away from his hold, Judith said: 'I suppose you mean you'll take the £500 instead,' moving towards the front door.

He looked at her in what seemed surprise, then dropping his hands to his sides, said vaguely: 'Oh yes.' He followed her to the door which she had now opened, then, having looked at her again in the same way, ran down the steps saying, impatiently: 'Oh yes yes yes yes yes yes. . . .'

The taxi grunted into movement as Feliks came out of the drawing-room behind her.

'Finished?' he asked.

'Yes,' said Judith.

'Do I understand that Jean-Claude is not leaving after all?' he asked. 'Or is Baldwin instead of me going to have him? You really must explain yourself a bit, Judith.'

'I'm afraid I can't altogether,' said Judith, turning back into the house.

8

Thomas Hood's aunt was anti-Semitic. She was also opposed to vivisection, and a believer in herb cures, but that was beside the point—it was her anti-semitism which her nephew could not forgive.

He was living, nevertheless, in her house in the Isle of Wight while his mother and sister were in America and their own house was shut up; although as a matter of fact he spent a good deal of time in London and arranged his visits to the Isle of Wight to coincide as much as possible with her absences, which were fortunately frequent. He did have David Weitzmann to stay once when she was there—two days of unrelieved embarrassment and gloom.

When he asked whether Judith might come down for a week-end, his aunt was pleased. She already knew a good deal about her, since even to so uncongenial an audience Thomas had not been able to avoid talking about her, and though at first she had been inclined to think the friendship not suitable, she had lately—without much evidence and mainly because it was convenient—come to the conclusion that Judith was not 'that sort of woman'. There was also the advantage, especially after the trying experience of David Weitzmann, that, as she delicately pointed out to her maid: 'Mrs. Lane is not One of Those.'

The maid, who used that term to denote the homosexual, said with some scorn: 'Indeed, no, ma'am, her being a lady.'

Taking this as a perfectly natural expression of aristocratic prejudice, Miss Hood said: 'Well of course the Lanes are a very good family, and I expect the boy would have married someone nice, don't you?'

Permission having been granted, Thomas then arranged for Judith to come down for the one weekend he was sure that his aunt would be away until Sunday night. 'I'm so sorry, it's the only one she can manage,' he told Miss Hood, untruthfully.

His reason for making this arrangement was partly because he himself found his aunt boring and would rather have Judith to himself, but mainly because he was ashamed of his aunt for being snobbish and unintelligent, and thought that Judith would despise him for having such a foolish relation. In this, of course, he was quite wrong, because Miss Hood was kind and jolly and Judith would have liked her, but he always expected of Judith opinions much more ruthless and uncompromising than her real ones. Also he set himself, in regard to her, an impossibly high standard.

He waited for her alone, then, in Miss Hood's comfortable Victorian house, walking occasionally out into the garden where the mimosa was already over, and wandering once down the lane to where the sea plopped on to the sand with a melancholy he had always liked. Throughout his childhood, this had been the place where his busy parents had sent their children for holidays or when there was for the moment nowhere else for them to go, and the soft sea of the island's northern coast and the stretch of sand where no one came except in August—and even then not in such crowds as went elsewhere, for there were better beaches near—and the strong scent of the ginger plants his aunt grew, and the ugly sweet-smelling house, were all part of his youth and full for him of the nostalgia which at nineteen he felt for the conflicts of sixteen.

When at last he went to fetch the car to meet Judith at Ryde pier head, he was full of quiet reasonable excitement.

Judith on the boat coming towards him was tired and rather cross. She was sick of Baldwin Reeves. She had thought of him almost without ceasing since he had brought Jean-Claude back to her house. He stayed in her mind with a deadly persistence, he was simply there: it was as if they were chained in some dungeon together, out of reach but face to face; to break away was impossible.

The point was that, for a moment in the hall of her house, she had thought he might kiss her and had wished that he would. Afterwards, shaken, she had tried, and failed, to persuade herself that this was not so. That night she had dreamt, dispensing with the subtleties of symbolism, that they were in bed together.

Having had since her husband had died only the slightest and most fleeting of sexual interests in any men, that her desires should now apparently have been aroused by a man she had thought she regarded with loathing seemed to her wicked. Sex and love had never been dissociated in her mind; nor altogether had love and liking, for though she had known Anthony's most serious faults, she would still, she felt, have liked him, in any circumstances, for his charm and wit and understanding: but Baldwin Reeves was a very different affair—he was practically the only man in the world whom she seriously had reason to hate.

Her instinct was to say: 'Nonsense,' but she was too honest to believe it could all be thus dismissed. In that case, the thing must be ignored, repressed, subdued—of course; but secretly her fatalism made her feel that nothing could be done about it, nothing could be avoided, the future was revealed.

She arrived then at Ryde feeling sad, restless and faintly depraved. At the same time she was very annoyed with Bertie, who had behaved horribly in the train because of a couple in the carriage who ate chocolate all the time, and had then escaped from her on the boat, got himself shut in the gentlemen's lavatory and there become hysterical.

'You're tired,' Thomas said in the car. 'You shall go straight to bed with a glass of milk and a biscuit.'

'What, no dinner?' said Judith.

'Perhaps a little if you promise to talk to me and not think of anything else at all,' said Thomas.

'Oh,' said Judith. 'Isn't the food very good?'

'It is rather good as a matter of fact,' said Thomas. 'There's a curious neurotic old cook left over from the good old days.'

'Neurotic?' asked Judith.

'A religious maniac,' said Thomas. 'And methylated spirits. But there's a boat we can go out in if you like. Tomorrow, I mean. Everyone's very serious about sailing here, but of course it hasn't started properly yet. We could fish.'

'Is she a serious sailing woman, your aunt?' asked Judith.

'She's too old,' said Thomas. 'She has rheumatism and puts garlic on it, but she used to sail. She's not here now, though. She's not coming back until Sunday. Didn't I tell you?'

'No,' said Judith.

'It will really be much nicer without her,' said Thomas. 'She's very boring and narrow-minded. David came down, did I tell you? It was disastrous.'

'No, tell me,' said Judith.

She had been thinking on the way down that the week-end would be nice for Bertie, and that it would be good for her too to be out of London, as long as the aunt was not too dull, but now that she had seen him again she remembered that she was fond of Thomas and that his company was always pleasant.

They sailed and fished. The sun shone, though it was still cold in the mornings and evenings. They played tennis, at which Thomas turned out to be very good. They ate a good deal, and played rough games with Bertie on the lawn. Thomas talked.

'Why have I no secrets from you, and you have obviously hundreds from me?' he asked.

'For one thing, I like listening,' said Judith. 'For another, such secrets as I have are either boring or inexpressible, and anyway I sometimes find it difficult to talk to you because I think that you think that I am different from what I am. And then of course you ask so many questions.'

'Which makes you not want to answer?' asked Thomas.

'Which makes me not bother to tell you things because I know you're bound to ask, in time,' she said.

'How are you different from what I think?' he asked. 'Less good?'

'Oh, I should think so,' she said.

'But you needn't worry,' he said. 'I know you're less good than I think, but I still think it.'

When Aunt Susan came back on Sunday evening, Judith was easily persuaded to stay until the next day, and Thomas's confidence after the two days they had already spent together was such that he hardly once blushed for his aunt.

On Saturday morning, Judith had written to Sir Ralph to tell him of the need for more money, but once that was done she almost forgot about the whole thing. Even the image of Baldwin Reeves retreated, to emerge occasionally for a moment or two, but without the same oppressive power.

'I'm coming up next week,' said Thomas, when he drove her to catch the boat. 'On Tuesday. I'll come and see you, shall I?'

When she said good-bye to him, Judith kissed him on the cheek. It was not a gesture she was much given to making but it seemed obvious. He looked pleased.

As the boat moved away she leant over the rail to wave to him, the morning being fine and sunny.

Feliks greeted Judith with some petulance when she went into the office.

'All this about my being your greatest friend,' he said. 'And you leave me completely out of your confidence. What's it all about? If it was Baldwin Reeves who was forcing you to send Jean-Claude away, why couldn't you tell me? You told me on Thursday that you'd decided he must go at once, and would I have him for a fortnight, which naturally I said I would. But you know how I hate being left in the dark. You might have told me. Why did Baldwin want him to go, anyway?'

'I've no idea,' said Judith. 'Honestly, Feliks, the whole thing was so complicated and so mad, that I simply couldn't go into it all.'

'Then why did he suddenly bring him back?' said Feliks.

'I don't know,' said Judith. 'I really don't know why he does anything.'

'Is he asking you for money still?'

'Yes.'

'What a monster he is,' said Feliks.

'I don't know,' said Judith. 'Perhaps he isn't. I just don't know.'

'Of course he's a monster,' said Feliks. 'I shall tell him so.'

'You mustn't let him know I've told you about it,' said Judith.

'Of course I shan't,' said Feliks. 'I shall simply tell him he's a monster. Now listen, *Skin Deep* having done so well, and what with one thing and another, I think we ought to have another secretary.'

'Oh, d'you think so really?' said Judith. 'I don't mind typing my own letters now and then, and Fisher's getting awfully good.'

'Fisher's not meant to be a typist,' said Feliks. 'He may look like one, but that's neither here nor there. No, the other night at Gavin Miller's party—now *that* you see after all I do owe entirely to Baldwin Reeves, we mustn't forget that—anyway, there I met quite a nice little girl called Sally Mann, and she seemed perfectly intelligent and wants a job and. . . .'

'Feliks,' said Judith. 'Don't pretend that you don't know perfectly well that her name is Lady Sarah Mann.'

'Well, but Judith,' said Feliks. 'But listen. She could be useful. She really could. She doesn't want much in the way of wages, and if she turned out to be good, you never know, if she's got a bit of money. . . .'

'You think her name would look good on the paper,' said Judith.

'I told her the whole thing depended on you,' said Feliks. 'She's quite clever. Incidentally, this man Ivor Jones—would you like me to have another look at the manuscript?'

'Oh dear,' said Judith. 'I sometimes think we conduct this office in a very unbusinesslike way.'

Ivor Jones was an enthusiastic Welshman whose novel Judith wanted to publish because she thought he would one day write a good one. Feliks, on the other hand, had until then been opposed to it on the grounds that too many of their writers were in the nature of long-term investments.

'I'll think about it,' said Judith, sighing. 'I'll think about it all.'

'You look tired,' said Feliks. 'How are you?'

'Oh, I'm all right,' said Judith. 'Perhaps I need a holiday. What about my going away for a week or two? I haven't for ages.'

Feliks smiled. 'Well, perhaps if we get another secretary . . .' he said.

'We'll get her,' said Judith. 'Where is she?'

'Oh, darling, how wonderful of you,' said Feliks. 'I'll get her to come in tomorrow and you can see what you think.'

Travel was the thing, Judith thought. Even a week-end with Thomas Hood had momentarily taken away her horror of Baldwin. That was the answer, simply geography, simply physical distance. It had been some time since its fascination had worked on her. When she had been younger it had always been on her mind. Not that she was so anxious to see new places— it was the departure more than the arrival which had appealed to her then. Simply to go. She thought again, making her way home from the office, of departure, of trains drawing slowly out of stations, and ships swaying away from crowded quays, of disciplined embarkations on to aeroplanes, of luggage, newspapers and odd encounters, of the infinite variety of individuals even now, even this evening, undertaking voyages.

When she reached home, she found Baldwin Reeves waiting for her.

He had made a fool of himself. The scene when he had brought Jean-Claude back to Judith had been simply absurd. His consciousness of this made him feel, as he always did when the possibility arose of his being laughed at, that the best thing to do would be simply to drop the whole business. He had had £400 out of it, and it was important to know when to stop. He was annoyed by Judith's having, as it seemed to him, insisted on offering him more money in exchange for Jean-Claude. He had come back, then, to tell her that he was not asking for more; and that his plan was simply to get out. The whole thing had become too complicated, and was best forgotten as soon as possible. In a way, he rather blamed Judith for his having turned out to be a not altogether successful blackmailer. It had shaken his faith in himself.

To Judith the sight of him was simply doom; and the look on her face amazed him. She had no idea why he had come, but felt quite convinced that he would never go.

'I came to say,' Baldwin began. 'That there seemed last time to be some misunderstanding about the money. Do you remember?'

'Yes, I remember,' said Judith.

'You seemed to think I wanted £500,' said Baldwin.

'Yes,' said Judith.

'I never said that,' said Baldwin. 'I don't know why you thought I had.'

'What d'you mean?' asked Judith.

'I never said I wanted £500.' said Baldwin.

'Oh,' said Judith.

'I don't,' said Baldwin. 'I don't want it.'

'You don't want it?' repeated Judith.

'No.'

'What? Never?' asked Judith.

'I told you the whole thing was only temporary,' said Baldwin.

'Oh,' said Judith. 'Well——' She began to move slowly about the room, nervously picking things up off the tables and putting them down again, moving a cushion, straightening a rug with her foot. Baldwin, standing in front of the fireplace, said nothing. Bertie had hurried downstairs to see about his evening meal.

'Well——' said Judith.

'I thought I'd better tell you,' said Baldwin.

'Yes,' said Judith.

'I'll go then,' said Baldwin, suddenly making for the door.

'Oh, but——' said Judith.

'Yes?' Baldwin paused.

'Nothing,' said Judith. 'I mean I had actually made arrangements—for the money.'

'I see,' said Baldwin. 'But surely, those sort of arrangements are quite easily changed?'

'Yes,' said Judith. 'I suppose so. You mean—it's the end—of the blackmailing I mean?'

'Oh yes yes yes,' said Baldwin, impatiently, going out into the hall.

Judith followed him in silence, and passing him put out her hand to open the front door. He put his hand on her arm to prevent her, then kissed her.

After the first shock, and the first acute pleasure, Judith found herself prolonging the kiss because she could not think of what to say after it. She drew back.

'We understand each other,' said Baldwin, who looked shaken. 'You must see, we understand each other, even when we don't want to. Haven't you felt that?'

Judith, nodding, allowed her head to incline towards, though not actually rest upon, his shoulder. He gave a small moan, and would have kissed her again. The moan, however, had been a mistake: it jarred, and Judith, anyway calmer, suddenly pushed him away.

'No, you must go,' she said. She looked at him for a moment, then smiled slightly—a smile in which she seemed to appeal to him to join. Then she opened the front door and said again: 'You must go.'

After a moment he said: 'Yes, I'll go,' without answering her smile.

He walked away from her quickly, angry with himself, not because of the kiss, which impetuous though it had been he certainly did not regret, but because of the moan he had made, which had been the cause of her pushing him away. She had been quite right, and for the first time he not only admired, he really respected her. It was not the way in which he was used to women behaving, but he was quite aware himself of its having been an insincere moan, and as such an insult to her intelligence. Yet he hated to think she believed him to be altogether insincere; it was merely that he was used to exaggerating his emotions on such occasions, in order by simulating a passion to engender one, both in himself and in the other person. In this case, however, he realised that he had been wrong, and it made him feel rather shabby.

In retrospect his mistake became more and more embarrassing. The hateful little sound seemed hideously vulgar: it was the sort of thing Anthony Lane would never have done.

The money would be coming all the same—that Judith knew. If there was one person on whom, ever since she had met him, she had relied, it was Sir Ralph.

Her father in his lifetime had been, though rather distant, upright and unfailingly kind; but her mother she remembered as having been hysterical and over-effusive, and there had been no one else, even Anthony, in whom there had ever been any question of her seriously putting her trust. Partly, of course, she was naturally self-reliant, partly the effect on her of her emotional embarrassing mother had been to breed in her a deep reserve.

With Sir Ralph, however, the reserve, in a curious way, was not there. It was not that she knew him so very well. Their relationship was the artificial but charming one between an old man, to a certain extent worldly, and the pretty girl his grandson had married; but she had felt immediately at ease with him, as if, if revelations had to be made, she would prefer them to be made to him. He had still his old charm, and she found his eccentricities amazingly sane. She was also aware that into her feeling for him there entered the consideration of who he was, that is to say of the people he had known, the houses he had stayed in, the line of similar ancestors. She was outside his world, or what his world had been, not so much even by birth or upbringing as by sentiment, and that made her see it round him as a mysterious but appealing attribute. If she had been told her attitude was snobbish, she would have been furious, but it probably was. There was more to it, however, than that—he was a symbol to her of more than merely a class.

He had a way, a partly defensive way, of seeming vague and forgetful. His great age and his constant state of disagreement with his daughter-in-law had made him now a little sly. Judith was right, all the same, in thinking him worthy of trust: he had never been anything else. Only, now, though the instincts and unquestioning reactions were still there, sometimes the means of putting them into effect, of safeguarding the trust or defending the faith, were lacking.

He had made a note in his little book of the payment to Judith for Baldwin Reeves, and had just sent her the money. One afternoon when his daughter-in-law came in to tell him that tea was ready, he was bent over his books, working out, in anticipation of the next demand, which account could least stand the strain of another payment and would therefore be the most satisfying to use, in order to alarm his bank manager.

'Tea's ready, Fa,' Mrs. Lane said. 'Nanny made it rather early I'm afraid; her watch was fast. Oh, you haven't seen your letters.' She picked up the afternoon post which was lying unnoticed by his desk. 'Here you are—the *Investor's Chronicle* and a letter from the Agricultural people—oh, and one from Judith. Shall I open it? It must be about the week-end.'

'Do, my dear, do,' said Sir Ralph. 'Subtract this from that and there we are. I'll come along in a moment, just got to finish this.'

'Couldn't you finish it afterwards?' said Mrs. Lane. 'You've got all the evening. What's this Judith says? I don't understand. What £500?'

'What's that?' said Sir Ralph.

I'm so terribly grateful that you can deal with the £500, Mrs. Lane read out. *I really believe it will be the last he'll ask for—I'm almost certain of this. You've no idea how much happier I've been about it since I've known you know. I knew Anthony well, always. . . .* 'What is this, Fa?' *though it made no difference to us.* What does she mean. . . . *but you would hardly believe the relief I feel because you understood him too. So you must see how really thankful I am.* . . . 'and so on. What on earth is she talking about? What is this, Fa? What an extraordinary letter.'

Sir Ralph pushed his chair back from his desk.

'May I have it please?' he asked.

He took the letter and gazed at it for some moments in silence. 'Twenty-fourth,' he said eventually. 'Ah yes, let's see, that was yesterday, wasn't it? Is there a postmark?'

'That's hardly important, Fa,' said Mrs. Lane. 'Do you mind explaining what this letter is about?'

'My dear, it was addressed to me,' said Sir Ralph, gently.

'You asked me to open it,' said Mrs. Lane. 'What is she talking about? What is it to do with Anthony?'

'It's nothing, nothing,' said Sir Ralph. 'There's no mystery, it's just a private matter. It's not important.'

'How can it be private when it concerns my son?" said Mrs. Lane.

Sir Ralph looked at her reproachfully.

'Judith and I sometimes correspond, you know,' he said. 'If she talks about her late husband to me, I don't always tell you about it.'

Mrs. Lane looked at him for a moment almost wildly. Then she said: 'So you refuse to answer my question?'

'If you put it like that,' said Sir Ralph.

Nanny's large white face peered round the door.

'Oh, you're here,' she said sadly.

'We're just coming,' said Mrs. Lane. 'You start tea, Nanny.'

'I have started,' said Nanny. 'It's getting cold.'

'Oh come along then,' said Mrs. Lane, impatiently. 'Come along, Fa.'

'You go ahead, Grizel,' said Sir Ralph. 'I'll follow you in a moment. I must just finish this calculation—won't take me a moment.'

Mrs. Lane hesitated, then, shepherded by Nanny, went out of the room.

Sir Ralph picked up a pen in his slightly trembly hand (he always wrote with a relief nib), but he left his subtraction half finished, and sat without moving at his desk. Later Nanny came back and took him, quite firmly, to tea.

9

There can be no doubt but that Miss Vanderbank was a dear creature. There was her adored Hanescu flirting about with the new secretary, who looked like a Red Indian but turned out, as Miss Vanderbank freely admitted, to be full of good intentions; and yet, horribly as she suffered, she still performed her duties with her usual bouncing efficiency and most generously watched, encouraged and sighed over what she felt confident was a romance developing between Judith and Baldwin.

'He's taking her out to lunch again,' she said to Fisher. 'And d'you see the way he looks at her?'

'But she's so rude to him always,' said Fisher, who, relieved though he was that Baldwin's attentions had been diverted from Miss Vanderbank, still regarded him with a certain amount of distrust.

'That's just it,' said Miss Vanderbank, wisely. 'That just proves it.'

'Oh,' said Fisher.

He would have been even more puzzled had he seen them at lunch, for Baldwin, who had now decided quite simply to get to know Judith better, in order both to explain to himself the attraction she had for him and to study and somehow deal with the challenge she represented, was finding his task difficult, and it was certainly not made easier by Judith, who was never, at the best of times, much of a breaker of silences.

One of his difficulties, curiously enough, was the fact that he felt he already knew her very well. This, being the result of the necessarily intimate nature of the relationship between blackmailer and victim, was an embarrassment rather than anything else. He had resolved to take things slowly, and at first confined their meetings to a series of lunches. For a time he tried to start all over again, and to keep the conversation on the same sort of note it would have had had they only just met; but since, unlike Judith, he was not fundamentally at all a tactful person, this manœuvre was not successful and he abandoned it.

'What I like about you,' he said once, 'is that you're not altogether what you pretend. If you were really the good conventional straightforward creature you sometimes seem, would you associate with that scoundrel Hanescu?'

'He's not,' said Judith.

'Not wholly, perhaps,' said Baldwin. 'But mostly. I don't mean to say he runs his business dishonestly, but you know his whole method is—well, shall we say, corrupt?'

Judith defended him, as best she could, but Baldwin laughing, simply said: 'Oh, you won't admit it to me. But I know you admit it to yourself.'

'Do I really seem like that?' asked Judith. 'Conventional and straightforward?'

'Sometimes,' said Baldwin. 'Of course, I've always held that you're less intelligent than you seem—you're well-read and you've got a good clear judgment, and that makes one think there's more behind you—oh, now you're insulted, I love that.'

It was true that she prided herself on her intelligence and hated to have it slighted.

'No, but I think you choose to seem conventional because you wish to be—perhaps it's the Lane influence, I don't know,' said Baldwin. 'You want to seem as if you never have any doubt about what's right or wrong, and yet I think it's only by ignoring a moral problem that you make it seem, both to yourself and to outside observers, as if for you it doesn't exist. It makes you seem strong, but I'm not sure it isn't a sign of weakness. You have too much moral pride: I believe if something upset it, you might find yourself quite at sea.'

'You mean I think myself better than I am,' said Judith.

'Stronger,' said Baldwin.

'And what sort of thing, then,' she asked, coldly, 'do you see upsetting this false equilibrium?'

'Me, for instance,' said Baldwin. 'I think I might upset it.'

'You?' she said.

'You think I'm bad and yet you love me,' said Baldwin, enjoying his own analysis. 'I think this constitutes a difficult moral problem for you, and one which you are prepared to go all sorts of lengths not to have to face. Of course you knew Anthony wasn't altogether a worthy person, but you apparently got over that somehow. I am a more difficult case, a little too much more unworthy. You don't want to face it. That's what I mean by your equilibrium being upset. You might do something odd and violent. I am not sure, but nothing would surprise me.'

They sat side by side without speaking for some time, then Judith said quietly: 'I am afraid I hate you for being so over-confident and so mistaken.'

When she looked at him after a moment, she was surprised to see that he had turned red and that his eyes were full of tears; but she was wrong in thinking that her reaction had much hurt him, for he had not expected any other. It was merely that thinking about her had suddenly filled him with emotion.

After a pause he said: 'You are like your husband, you know. It's funny, isn't it, that someone so weak of character should be so powerful of personality? I've no doubt he influenced you more than you did him.'

'I'm sure he did. I never knew what were the influences in his life. There were none that I could recognise.'

'Perhaps he was always self-sufficient,' said Baldwin. 'There was something a little cold about it. Perhaps he never loved anybody enough to be much influenced by them.'

'Perhaps not,' she said gently.

Slightly embarrassed, Baldwin went on quickly: 'He influenced me, of course, enormously. The way I talk, I mean the actual words I use, inflexions, intonations, all come from him.'

'I know,' she said.

They talked about Anthony a good deal: neither of them had talked about him much with anybody before. At those times they were not so defensive with each other; but usually their meetings were sharply quarrelsome. Baldwin found them exciting and stimulating, Judith, for the same reasons, frightening. It had not occurred to him that if it was power he was after he might do better by being nice to her. He was delighted to find it out, but she was for the first time really worried by him.

She began to avoid him with more of a sense of oppression and fear than she had ever had while he was blackmailing her.

One evening he came into the office just as she was leaving. 'I was on my way home so I thought I'd pick you up,' he said.

Miss Vanderbank fluttered past in a chiffon scarf, smiling blissfully. Baldwin found himself quite grateful for her so obvious blessing.

They took Bertie into the park. Baldwin had just secured an extremely good brief, in fact he had made what could fairly be considered something of a coup. He would have told her about it, but then somehow he did not tell her, and the fact of his silence gave him pleasure, because he knew she thought him boastful and this was surely a proof to the contrary.

When they reached Judith's house, Thomas Hood was waiting in the drawing-room. Judith was so relieved to see him that she greeted him with too much enthusiasm.

'Oh, Thomas! How simply wonderful to see you!' she cried, and stood smiling delightedly at him.

Thomas looked a little surprised, and then shook her hand, and Baldwin's, in his punctilious way.

Baldwin, on whom Judith's unusual enthusiasm had not been lost, answered without much grace, and sat down aggressively.

Judith suddenly unleashed a flood of idle talk, which was

received with complete silence by Baldwin and with a polite response but a look of mild concern by Thomas. Baldwin was relieved when the telephone rang, because it put a stop to this chatter which annoyed and puzzled him.

'Mrs. Lane?' a husky voice said, with so outrageous cockney cum Scottish accent that Judith thought at first it must be Feliks, who had a liking for that sort of telephoning. She was wrong, however.

'Sandy's the name,' said the voice. 'Pal of Jimmy's—Jimmy Chandos-Wright—yes, that's it. Said you might be wanting me for a job. Well, he did say there'd maybe a spot of delay—I thought I'd just let you know I'm free. Got a job on next month though. Could fit yours in before that if you like? No? Quite sure of that, are you? Always ready to oblige a friend, you know. Tell you what, I'll give you a number where you can get me, shall I? Then we can cut out the middleman, eh? Not that I mean I'd do Jimmy out of his lick—not an old pal like Jimmy—but saves time, eh? Should you come to be in a hurry, see?'

'Thank you so much—yes—thank you—good-bye. . . .' She put down the receiver. 'No, really, it's too much,' she said. 'Too much. I can't bear it.'

'What's too much?' Thomas stood up.

'The whole thing,' Judith said. 'No, I mean everything——No, really, why should I?'

'Should you what?' said Thomas.

'Anything,' said Judith, 'I mean, really. . . .'

Thomas led her to a chair. 'Take your coat off and sit down,' he said. 'You're talking nonsense. Sit down. There you are. You really mustn't get so excited. That's right.'

Baldwin Reeves stood up angrily. 'I'd better go,' he said. 'I don't seem to be sufficiently soothing. Good-bye Judith.'

'Good-bye,' said Judith.

As soon as he had gone, she turned to Thomas and cried: 'Oh, why did you make him go?'

'You are in a state,' said Thomas. 'What shall I do for you?'

'I'm sorry, Thomas, I really am,' she said. 'Oh dear, how

awful of me. I don't know what it is. I ought to go away or something.'

'What you want,' said Thomas, 'is a nice quiet holiday by the sea, with plenty of fresh air, exercise and good food. Isn't it? So we'll go down to the Isle of Wight tomorrow. Aunt Susan's away and you can do whatever you like. I'll ring up tonight and say we'll be there in time for tea.'

'Oh, d'you think so?' said Judith.

'Of course,' said Thomas.

'Well, yes,' said Judith. 'It is kind of you. No, I don't want a handkerchief thank you.'

'Bother,' said Thomas, putting it away.

'Why?' asked Judith.

'I often imagine you crying and me comforting you,' said Thomas.

'Oh do you?' said Judith. 'I'm sure it's not in the least like this.'

'Yes, it is,' said Thomas. 'Only you cry more.' He went to telephone his aunt's house.

In the morning Judith told Feliks that she would like to take advantage of the new secretary's presence to take a week off, and they went down to the Isle of Wight.

It was warmer than before. There were a few little sailing boats fluttering about the sea, and one great lovely schooner stretching new sails. The trees were all out and some early azaleas. The daffodils were already over. On the sheltered part of the beach, two or three groups of children built sand castles, and three more fortunate ones daily galloped past on tubby uncontrollable ponies. Farther along it was rocky and deserted. They walked there one day, and Bertie chased seagulls and fell into the sea. After that he began to like it and took to sea-bathing with an enthusiasm astonishing in one so luxury-loving. Judith was happy and guilty—guilty about Thomas, about Baldwin, about herself. Baldwin still lurked in her mind, and his presence there made her feel all the more strongly that there was something in what she was doing now, in her respite, in Thomas, to be snatched at while there was still time.

'You're better,' Thomas said. 'Aren't you?'

'Yes,' she smiled.

'You remember you were going to let me know when you felt like love?' he said.

'Was I?' she said.

'Of course,' he said. 'I think it's probably about now, don't you?'

'No, I don't think so,' she said. But she let him kiss her, and the love which she recognised in him touched her, and made her realise how much she needed it, how much difference already, in spite of her other unhappiness, his love had made to her. She meant to feel ashamed of herself, but somehow could not, and returned his kiss.

He got up, took her hand, and led her out of the room.

'Where are we going?' she asked, but he did not answer and led her upstairs to her bedroom.

'You can put your clothes on that chair,' he said, shutting the door. 'And I'll have this one.'

She meant to laugh, or protest, or ask questions, but before his solemnity she said nothing, but undressed quietly and got into bed.

After that the figure of Baldwin Reeves did not retreat but became less menacing. She felt it all to be only a suspension of time, but she could not deny that for the moment she was happy, and that everything Thomas did helped to make her more happy.

Thomas himself was wholly in love. Obscurely he felt he should not tell her: he hardly knew why—it was perhaps an attempt at what he felt was sophisticated behaviour, perhaps a dim fear which he would not yet admit to himself that words might show up the difference in their states of mind. So sometimes tears would run down his face and though he might sob, or hurt her, or stare enraged into her eyes, he still said nothing. Partly, of course, he did not know the words. His experience of love, though it was more extensive than that of his contemporaries who had not been brought up, as he had been, abroad—that is to say, though it included having once been to bed with a woman—had not taught him its vocabulary. He could say 'darling' but when he once said 'my darling' he blushed furiously and never tried it again.

Judith never knew the extent of his feelings. She realised that he loved her, that he was very moved, that he had known nothing like it; but she never knew how all his life was now in terms of her, how he quite took it for granted that when he had been to Oxford he would marry her and live happily ever after. If she had thought she might have known, but she was, after all, fairly self-centred, and besides she did not want to think.

She was relieved that Thomas's questionings seemed to have come to an end, and that he said nothing about the future, nor did it occur to her that this was because he imagined there was no doubt about it. Sometimes lying beside her in the big spare bedroom he simply laughed, thinking about it. She would ask him why and he would refuse to tell her. Then she would take him by the shoulders and say: 'Tell me, tell me. . . .' and he would kiss her again, sometimes too roughly, so that she had to stop him, and then he would be sorry. Then he would make love to her again more gently, and then quite suddenly he would be asleep.

Behind his confidence there did lurk a small uncertainty, but he wanted to be confident, and nearly all the time he was.

They stayed longer than a week. Judith rang up her office, but was unable to take business problems in the least seriously. Hanescu, talking to her, sounded a little puzzled: indeed she spoke as if she were in Timbuctoo, not ninety miles away in a big Victorian villa in the Isle of Wight. But Aunt Susan came back, Thomas's mother and sister had finished their visit to America, and nothing could wait.

They travelled back to London and parted at the station, with peace of mind on Thomas's part and a great sense of loss on Judith's. She took a taxi to Chelsea, and as it turned into the street she saw the familiar figure of Baldwin on her doorstep. He was asking when she would be coming back, and she saw him, having been turned away by Jean-Claude, come down the steps and walk into the King's Road, preoccupied, passing her taxi without noticing who was in it.

'I'm going to ask you a question,' Mrs. Lane said. 'To which you needn't of course reply if you don't want to. But I feel you will, because I don't think, really, we've many secrets, have we?'

She was smartly dressed, as she always was, in London, and had had her hair done that morning—it was naturally wavy and fitted her fine small head in blue-grey exactitude. Her dark eyes bent their kind distant smile on Judith, a smile as controlled and calm as all her other manifestations.

A little frightened, Judith said: 'Of course we haven't.'

'No,' said Mrs. Lane, leaning back in her chair and accepting a cup of tea. 'It's just that poor old Fa—well, you know, really he's a bit past.'

Already anxious about what was to come, Judith wished her mother-in-law would not look so grand. Harris, Heaven knew, was shabby enough, yet for some reason Mrs. Lane always made Judith feel the little Chelsea house was hopelessly inadequate.

'He likes to make a mystery out of things,' Mrs. Lane went on. 'I suppose it's because, poor old thing, he hasn't much to occupy him these days.'

'No,' said Judith, now sure of what was coming.

'It was just a letter which he asked me to open for him,' said Mrs. Lane. 'One of yours. And there was some mention in it of Anthony, and a sum of money, which I didn't quite understand, and when I asked him he became so secretive that I thought the best thing was to ask you. I didn't want to worry him about it.'

'No, of course not.' Judith paused. 'Well, as a matter of fact, it is something, not really—well, which you might not like.'

She looked at the woman sitting opposite her. There seemed

to be so much strength in her face that Judith wondered whether she had not been foolish in not telling her before.

'If you want to know, of course I'll tell you,' she said. 'I didn't before because it's rather unpleasant.'

'If it concerns Anthony I should like to know it,' said Mrs. Lane.

'Well,' said Judith, reluctant to remind herself. 'I suppose I must.' She sighed. 'Anthony wasn't a very brave man. You probably know that. He had many more important qualities and it doesn't alter the fact that we all loved him. But the reports of how he behaved in Korea were not quite truthful.'

'They were perfectly well authenticated,' said Mrs. Lane.

'Somebody who had been with him the whole time came to see me,' said Judith. 'And told me the whole story—about how frightened Anthony had been. . . .'

'Frightened?' said Mrs. Lane. 'I imagine they were all frightened.'

'Somebody else had to take over the command,' said Judith. 'And Anthony kept back the order to retreat because he thought it was an order to stay where they were. And then in the prison camp some of them were treated very badly. Anthony gave away a plan to escape and so someone was shot. Anthony didn't die of wounds as it was said. He wasn't wounded.'

'He was shot trying to escape?' asked Mrs. Lane.

'He was killed by the other prisoners,' said Judith. 'Because he gave away their plan to escape and one of them was shot by the guards.'

Mrs. Lane put down her tea cup.

'Who told you this?' she asked.

'Someone who'd been with him,' said Judith. 'He blackmailed me, saying that he would make a public scandal out of it by telling the whole story to the newspapers. So I had to give him money.'

'Was it the man you told me about? Reed?' Mrs. Lane asked.

'No no, not him,' said Judith. 'Another man.'

'But this man Reed was with him,' said Mrs. Lane. 'He can deny the story.'

'Reeves,' said Judith. 'He said the same thing.'

'He was jealous,' said Mrs. Lane. 'He was always jealous. I knew at the time. He should never have been allowed in the regiment.'

Judith, who had not looked at her mother-in-law while she was speaking, now raised her eyes and saw that Mrs. Lane had turned a yellowish white. She did not meet Judith's eyes, but turning her face away said: 'Why did you not tell me at once?'

'I didn't want to tell you,' said Judith. 'I couldn't see any point in upsetting you.'

'Upsetting me?' said Mrs. Lane. 'Upsetting me? What an extraordinary thing to say. It doesn't upset me in the slightest.'

'It doesn't?' said Judith, amazed. 'Then you knew—we all knew—oh, how strange!'

'Of course I knew my son,' Mrs. Lane said. 'I knew him better than anyone else. I was the only person he cared for. I knew him, and I know him now.'

Judith said nothing.

Mrs. Lane went on, in a hard rasping voice that trembled frighteningly.

'I know that no amount of slander can make any difference. He was always brave and true and honourable—all his life. He came of a decent family, and he upheld its traditions. It was unthinkable to him to do anything dishonest. He was an English gentleman.'

Judith gave a sort of moan.

'You know it as well as I do,' said Mrs. Lane, in her new voice. 'How dare you take our money to pay some slanderer for his lies? It was wicked of you, wicked. The man must be punished. I shall go round to the War Office at once—yes, now.' She stood up. 'I'm going to put a stop to it at once. What is the name of this man? He wasn't there at all. I knew all of them who were with Anthony. What is his name?'

Judith got up too. 'Please. . . .' she began. 'Please don't do anything rash. I have thought so carefully about whether anything could be done. . . .'

'What is his name?' said Mrs. Lane.

'But please,' said Judith. 'It won't do any good.'

Mrs. Lane suddenly seized her by both arms. 'What is his name?' she said wildly. 'What is his name? What is his name?'

'But I can't tell you, I can't,' said Judith. 'He didn't tell me who he was. He wouldn't say.'

Mrs. Lane began to shake her. 'You'll tell me who he is,' she now spoke in a sort of screaming whisper. 'I'll make you tell me. I daresay you thought it all very fine to get money out of an old idiot like that. Didn't you? What did you do with the money? Did you keep it? Did you make the whole thing up?'

'No no stop,' said Judith. 'You mustn't say that. I know how awful it is. I was horrified too.'

'So you were horrified,' Mrs. Lane was still gripping Judith's arms. 'You were horrified. Oh yes. Of course. You thought it was a good way of getting money didn't you? Was it for this man, or did you make the whole thing up yourself? He's your lover—you hatched the plot between you. You've always been after our money. That's why you married Anthony. I knew at the time you didn't care for him.'

'Oh don't don't,' said Judith. 'You mustn't say that, you don't mean it.'

Mrs. Lane suddenly let go of her arms, pushing her violently away.

'You never understood him,' she walked away from Judith. 'You wanted the money, the position. I knew. How could you understand that sort of man, who was a gentleman and came from a good family? This could never have happened, never, when I was young. Nobody would have believed you then. The world's changed. People have no sense of values, no decency, they're all out for what they can get. Our sort of people get pushed aside by all the lies and ingratitude. The Welfare State —it's just a means of sheltering these liars and slanderers and upstarts. I brought Anthony up in the old-fashioned way, to be what his father was before him.'

She suddenly stopped, and turned fiercely round.

'If his father had been alive this would never have happened,' she said. 'He would never have allowed it. He wouldn't have allowed the marriage. He'd have seen Anthony married to someone who could understand him, someone of his own sort.' Tears began to run down her face, which did not change its expression of fierce despair. 'I spent my whole life in bringing up Anthony to be what he was. My whole life. My husband died of overwork for his country—they don't do that now. They have a five day week, holidays with pay, pensions, free this, free that. But my husband and my son died for them. They don't do anything for widows and mothers, do they, in the Welfare State? They don't do anything for me, do they? I have to live out my miserable life in that horrible uncomfortable house with a gaga old man, and who cares what becomes of me? I don't get anything for it. They don't do anything for old women, do they? Who ought to be being looked after. But who cares for what I've done for my country—both my brothers were killed in the war. But they don't do anything for old women. There's no sense of values. The young are so selfish. . . .' her voice mercifully began to die down.

'I know,' said Judith quickly, urgently wishing to put an end to this horrifying tirade. 'I know how you feel, I really do. . . . Look, do come and sit down.'

'You don't know anything,' said Mrs. Lane. 'You're selfish and hard like all your immoral generation. Why should I sit down, here, in your house, when you're a traitor to everything Anthony died for?'

Judith said gently: 'You needn't of course. I'm sorry. I didn't know there was all this bitterness in you—I never really knew what you were feeling, but I never imagined, I never dreamt, it could be this.'

Mrs. Lane was now leaning against the wall in an attitude of exhaustion, still very pale.

'You think I'm just a bitter old woman,' she said. 'You wait. You'll see. I've been patient. I've done my duty. But who cares for an old woman? I'm ugly. I'm often in pain. What do I get back for what I gave? Soon I shall die, but who'll care about that? I'm just a useless old woman in a world that's made for money, and war, and power. Nobody believes in what I believe in now.'

'But you must believe it,' Judith was trembling with shock and with desire to persuade this unknown frantic being out of its despair. 'You don't believe it any more. You haven't thought lately, you've forgotten what your faith was—it wasn't like this. It was strong and valid once. It was a faith in humanity and God, and. . . .'

'God!' said Mrs. Lane, jerking herself away from the wall and sitting slowly down in an armchair. 'What do you know about God? You're all atheists, your generation. Our God doesn't exist any more. You saw to that.' She took a small hand-kerchief out of her bag and blew her nose violently. 'What do you care about Anthony?' she then said. 'You never had any children. The modern generation don't believe in children. I know.'

The door was suddenly opened and Jean-Claude's ugly sane face looked in. 'You heard not the bell?' he asked. 'Is Mr. Reeves.'

'Oh Baldwin,' said Judith, as his figure appeared in the dark of the hall, behind Jean-Claude. 'Look, I've something to show you here, before you come in. . . .'

Outside the drawing-room she shut the door, and led Baldwin half way up the stairs, out of earshot.

'Listen, I've had the most terrifying scene with my mother-in-law,' she said quickly. 'About Anthony. I had to tell her—she found out—I can't explain now. But she went absolutely frantic, she won't believe it, she thinks I made it up to get the money—I can't tell you how awful it was. She's almost mad.'

'What can I do?' asked Baldwin. 'D'you want me to go?'

'No, we'll go in in a minute,' said Judith. 'It's better, I think. If she's alone with me she'll only start again. But she knows you were with Anthony. She doesn't think you're the black-mailer. I told her that was someone else; but she's very likely to talk to you about it.'

'What do you want me to say?' asked Baldwin.

'You must tell her he was a hero,' said Judith. 'It doesn't matter what she thinks of me. Tell her that.'

She led the way back into the drawing-room.

The arrival of a stranger had induced Mrs. Lane to make the effort necessary to calm herself. She was sitting quietly, looking at an evening paper. Judith introduced Baldwin, and he began to make polite conversation while Jean-Claude cleared away the tea things. Judith, suddenly tired, leant back in her chair and allowed Baldwin to take over the conversation. She had to admit he did it well, talking entertainingly but uncontroversially about theatres, the traffic problem, this and that. The look of strain lessened on Mrs. Lane's face, but after a time she took advantage of a brief pause to say, with her polite smile:

'Wasn't it you who was in the same regiment as my son Anthony?'

'Yes, that's it,' said Baldwin. 'I remember coming to your flat in Hyde Park Gate once with him. Have you still got that? It was so nice, I remember.'

'No, I gave it up,' said Mrs. Lane. 'I don't come up to London a great deal now. My life is much quieter without Anthony. We were so much together, you know.'

'Yes, of course,' said Baldwin. 'You live up in Lancashire, then, do you? Or is it Yorkshire?'

'Anthony was a wonderful son to me,' said Mrs. Lane, without answering. 'There aren't many people like that nowadays. They always say it's the best who go, don't they?'

Judith, checking an impulse desperately to agree, went over to the cupboard in the hope that an offer of a drink might change the subject.

'Didn't Judith tell me,' said Mrs. Lane. 'That you were with Anthony most of that terrible time?'

'Yes, I was,' said Baldwin.

'You'll forgive me if I say I think that was a privilege?' said Mrs. Lane, smiling again.

'It was,' said Baldwin. 'Anthony had immense charm. I very much enjoyed knowing him. He had a lot of friends, of course. I wonder if you ever see any of them. Do you remember Charles Finnigan, who came with us to the flat that day?'

'Some of his friends were rather odd,' said Mrs. Lane. 'Some were jealous, and wanted to detract from his glory. He died a glorious death, you see.'

'Yes,' said Baldwin. 'But Charles was always one of his most outspoken admirers. I just wondered whether you knew what he'd done after the war. His family lived in Leicestershire somewhere, I think.'

Miraculously, Mrs. Lane did know the Finnigans and could be persuaded to talk about them. In fact the conversation flowed on comparatively smoothly until she said, addressing Judith for the first time since Baldwin's arrival: 'I'm afraid I must go. The Digbys are back from Washington and very kindly asked me to dinner, and I shall have to change. I'm looking forward to seeing them again. Thank you so much for my tea. No, don't bother to see me out. Oh, my coat—thank you so much, Mr. Reed. I'm glad to think you knew Anthony. You know, mothers are foolish, I'm afraid, and I'm awfully proud to think he was a hero.' Again the wild smile, and she shook hands with Baldwin, though not with Judith, and was gone.

'Oh oh oh,' Judith sank into a chair. 'That was awful, terrible, frightful. . . .'

'She will convince herself again that he was a hero,' said Baldwin. 'She'll really believe it before long.'

'But what can her life be like?' said Judith. 'I had no idea, no idea. You don't know the bitterness she revealed, the horror. Bitterness against everything. Oh, such despair. . . .'

Baldwin sat down opposite her, and looked at her attentively. 'It's not easy to be old,' he said.

'But I had no idea,' said Judith. 'That's what's so extraordinary. Was she always like that, do you imagine?'

'Probably it was once quite an admirable pride,' said Baldwin.

'What are you doing here?' said Judith. 'I forgot about that. I couldn't bear another scene.'

'I'm very reasonable really,' said Baldwin, smiling. 'Very reasonable. If you like I'll go away, but I'd rather not.'

'No, it doesn't matter,' said Judith. 'Besides I'd rather not be alone—life's too alarming, suddenly.'

'What a confession,' said Baldwin. 'You admit that you'd rather have me than nothing—I never dared hope for as much as that. No, I mean it—it was a moment of weakness of which I won't remind you, but I am pleased.'

'But look,' said Judith. 'All this is your fault.'

'I know,' said Baldwin seriously. 'Of course I know. I want to talk to you about it, and about some other important things, but I thought perhaps not now?'

'No, not now,' said Judith. 'After dinner.'

'After dinner,' said Baldwin, noticing that she was committing herself to spending the evening with him.

'How did she find out?' he asked later.

'She opened a letter I wrote to the old man,' said Judith.

'What did it say?' asked Baldwin.

'Oh, it mentioned the money and so on,' said Judith. 'He paid it you see. The £500 came. I knew it would, and now you say you don't want it.'

'No,' said Baldwin. 'Send it back. I never knew you'd told him.'

'You told me to, don't you remember?' said Judith. 'I hadn't got that amount of money myself.'

'Oh,' said Baldwin.

'So now I'm to send it back?' asked Judith.

'Yes,' said Baldwin.

'Well, you have got into a mess, haven't you, over this?' said Judith.

'Yes,' said Baldwin.

'I can't think what you were doing really,' said Judith. 'And it was very dangerous. You might easily have gone to prison.'

'Perhaps that was what appealed to me about it?' suggested Baldwin.

'I don't think so,' said Judith.

'No,' said Baldwin. 'I think it was jealousy of Anthony among other things. He got away with so much, you know;

and then I felt he was even getting away with that, when I came back and found him a public hero. And you looked a bit like him, in a way, as if you might be equally unassailable. That made me want to tell you—yes, nasty I know. I knew it was nasty at the time. The thought of blackmail came second.'

'You felt that gave you a reasonable excuse for making the revelation which was to humiliate me?' asked Judith, coldly.

'Possibly, possibly,' said Baldwin. 'I don't fool myself. I did it only because I thought anything legitimate which might serve to further my ambitions.'

'You still think that?' asked Judith.

Baldwin looked embarrassed. 'It's a—a theory which might have to be modified,' he said. 'In practice.'

Judith smiled.

'But you can imagine feeling the power,' he said, with some vehemence, looking at her. 'The power in you. Imagine feeling every day more confident in it, knowing it's growing and time is passing, and not being allowed to use it.'

'There's humility,' said Judith. 'The most tiresome, and the most often misinterpreted, of the Christian virtues, I know, but still there it is.'

'I have no humility and no patience,' said Baldwin. 'Perhaps you would care to teach them to me.'

'I don't think I can teach you anything,' said Judith.

He was not prepared to argue with her now. He smiled and said: 'You taught me how not to be a blackmailer.'

'I should have thought you were quite a successful one,' said Judith.

'You mean the money?' he said. 'You must tell me which was his and which was yours, so that I can return it.'

'And that, of course, will make everything all right?' said Judith.

'I know, I know,' he said. 'I told you. I made you tell him. And the mother.'

'She'll never get over it,' said Judith. 'And he is a simple man with simple principles who—what an awful thing to have done, what an awful thing.'

'Yes,' said Baldwin. 'It was irresponsible. You know I wish you hadn't told him. I never really thought you would.'

'How was I to get the money?' said Judith. 'And there you were, waving that foul document in front of my face. No, you can't shift the blame.'

'I wasn't trying to do that,' said Baldwin. 'No, I accept it all. But it makes it difficult. He knows it's me, of course?'

'Yes,' said Judith.

'Yes,' he said. 'No, I really wish he didn't know. I really wish he didn't.'

'Why?' said Judith. 'What does it matter to you?'

'It makes things difficult,' said Baldwin. 'Especially in view of the proposition I was going to make to you. You're fond of him, aren't you?'

'What proposition?' asked Judith.

'You respect his opinion, don't you?' said Baldwin. 'He's your family, more or less, only you're more sentimental about him. Isn't that so?'

'I suppose so,' said Judith. 'It's my home, very much. There's no reason why it should be, now, but it still is.'

'And you go up for a lot of week-ends,' said Baldwin. 'And you really rather admire your mother-in-law too. And there's old Nanny, and the house, and the village.'

'Did I tell you this?' asked Judith.

'Not in so many words,' he said.

'What about it?' she said.

'I'm afraid if we got married it might mean a break with them,' he answered.

There was a pause. 'I should have thought that was a contingency which was hardly likely to arise,' said Judith, eventually.

'You don't face facts,' he said.

'Facts?' she echoed.

'The fact of—no, don't be angry—the fact of what exists between us,' he said. 'Please don't ignore it. But we should get on very well. We're the same sort of person. Together we should be much more of a force than apart.'

'You're thinking of power again,' she said. 'You think I might help you to be successful—a wife might be useful to your career. I'm to be nice to the right people, have them to dinner, open fêtes and jumble sales when you stand for Parliament.'

He smiled. 'You'd be rather good at it,' he said. 'You'd hate it, but funnily enough you'd really be quite good at it. No, you know I don't mean only that: you want to pretend I mean that so that you can work yourself up into a rage and think how despicable I am, but there's more to it than that, and I know you know it because you always know what I mean. That you can admit—aren't I horribly clear to you?'

'I suppose so,' she said.

'Look, you know how you find the world,' he said. 'Remember that scene tonight with Mrs. Lane. You know how sometimes madness seems to be on every side. You see it on people's faces in the street. Or illness. You think everything's fine with people and then there's some little lie and the whole thing's gone to pieces. Sometimes you think the only people who aren't impossibly shifty or mad are the very very stupid, or the ones who are dying. But you and I, to each other, are different. We're reasonable, we're of the same mind—we haven't altogether proved it, but we know it. We do, you know.'

'I don't,' said Judith. 'Nor do I think all that.' She was thinking of Thomas, but rather as if he were dead.

'You think I'm bad, you know,' said Baldwin, after a pause. 'With reason, no doubt. But what about you? You seem, in some curious way, to have come to think of yourself as a Lane —not a member of the real Lane family, because after all we both know the very great weaknesses of that—but a sort of idealised Lane, upholding the old traditions, rooted firmly in your county past, a part of English history. . . .'

'No,' said Judith. 'Nonsense.'

'Now morally,' said Baldwin. 'I'm the first to admit you're a good deal better than I am, but you can be unscrupulous too. What about your behaviour to Thomas Hood? How's that been?'

'What d'you mean?' she said.

He paused, then said: 'Well, we won't go into it. All I mean. . . .'

'Yes we will,' she said. 'What about Thomas Hood?'

'No, you looked guilty,' he said. 'It doesn't matter.'

'Yes it does,' she said. 'What are you talking about?'

'Oh, my dear, what do I know about it?' he said. 'I've seen you together that's all. I've seen him, after that time you went away for so long. I know you used him as an escape from me. I know the state of mind you were in. I can see he's in love with you, as you are not with him, and that you know he's very young and quite unable to deal with you. I can only think your behaviour rather ruthless.'

Judith's eyes filled with tears but she said nothing.

'He can't help, you know,' said Baldwin. 'It's no good pretending things are other than they are. That's why I think we ought to get married.'

After a pause, Judith said: 'Apart from anything else, you've already pointed out that it would mean the end of any sort of relations with the Lanes. That makes it out of the question for me.'

'Will you try one thing?' said Baldwin. 'And if it fails you shall decide as you like. Take me up there for a week-end. She doesn't know I was the blackmailer. I'll return the money to you, so that you can pay him back before we go there, and we'll explain to him somehow that it was a mistake and I'll see if I can improve the situation. Just let me try. After that, if you really want it, I'll give up.'

'You really will?' she said.

'Yes,' he answered.

'I suppose I could,' she said, slowly. 'If you insist. I could ask anyway. Yes, I suppose I could.'

'You will then?' he asked.

'Yes, I will,' she said. 'All right. I will.'

Thomas's mother and sister came back from America. He went to meet the boat train at Victoria.

On the station he bought two yellow rosebuds, one for each

of them. When he had come out of the shop he stood uneasily between platforms six and seven, holding the flowers and wondering if the gesture were not rather affected. He decided it was. He would rather keep them and give them to Judith; but he could hardly greet his mother and Emma holding flowers which were not for them. If he shortened their stalks, he might almost put them in his pocket; but then they would probably be squashed. Could he, perhaps, out of the two pieces of paper in which they were severally wrapped, make them into one uninteresting parcel which would escape his mother's notice?

Engrossed in this problem, he began to walk towards the platform at which the boat train would arrive.

A moment later he saw Baldwin Reeves. He would have preferred not to have spoken to him, but Baldwin had already seen him, and breezily accosted him.

'Ah Thomas!' he said. 'Where are you off to? I'm on my way back from a case in the suburbs—you've no idea what lurid lives they lead there. What charming flowers.'

'I'm meeting my mother,' said Thomas. 'She's coming back from America.'

'I wonder how it will have affected your nice sister,' said Baldwin. 'They've been there several months haven't they?'

'Three,' said Thomas.

'Seen anything of Judith Lane lately?' said Baldwin.

'Yes,' said Thomas.

The proud monosyllable annoyed Baldwin. Not having altogether meant to, he nevertheless found himself saying: 'We're getting married you know.'

Thomas looked surprised, and politely interested.

'Congratulations,' he said.

Baldwin was embarrassed, and would have liked to have withdrawn his remark.

He went on rather abruptly: 'Yes, we're going up there next week-end—tomorrow in fact. Well, I must be going—see you later.'

'Up where?' asked Thomas.

'To Harris,' said Baldwin.

'Oh I see,' said Thomas, with more interest. 'Is she a friend of Judith's?'

'Is who a friend of Judith's?'

'Your—that is, the person you are marrying?'

'But I am marrying Judith.'

They stood without moving, Baldwin half turned away and Thomas amazed.

'I don't understand you,' said Thomas, eventually.

Baldwin moved his feet awkwardly. 'I'm afraid I've been a bit premature in telling you,' he said.

'No, no,' said Thomas. He paused a moment, then went on firmly: 'But there's a mistake. You're wrong.'

Baldwin smiled uneasily, annoyed again. 'I'm not, you know,' he said.

'You can't marry Judith,' said Thomas, with finality.

'I can,' said Baldwin. There was another pause.

'Judith is my mistress,' said Thomas.

Baldwin turned red. 'Even so. . . .' he said.

'She told you?' asked Thomas.

'Well. . . .' said Baldwin.

'How can you marry her, then?' said Thomas.

'Look, I'm awfully sorry about this,' said Baldwin.

'How can you marry her?'

'What do you mean, how can I?' said Baldwin. 'Of course I can.'

'I don't understand,' said Thomas.

'I'm sorry,' said Baldwin. 'I should have left it to her to tell you.' He stood inadequately, not knowing what to say but not thinking of telling Thomas the truth, that he had simply made the suggestion to Judith. This was because, though he felt genuinely sorry for Thomas, it seemed to him out of the question that he should lose face in front of him by going back on his original assertion: he was also by now convinced that it would soon become a fact.

'Well, I must be getting along, you know,' he said. 'Sorry about all this. Silly of me to say anything about it. Anyway— we'll meet soon. Good-bye.'

But Thomas, though almost as outwardly composed as ever, was in the grip of the most bitter emotion of his life. Out of it he said, suddenly and loudly as Baldwin began to walk away, 'I want you to have these.'

He held out his two yellow roses, stiffly, at the end of his arm. Baldwin stopped, but looked at him in silence. Thomas pressed the roses into his hand, stared into his face a little wildly, and in a moment had disappeared, running through the crowd towards the way out of the station.

II

They went to Harris. It was May and bitterly cold. The wind from the north swept through Wensleydale and Wharfedale, whisking away, it is true, the rainy edges of the deep cloud that lay over the Lake District, but bringing with it a bleak unseasonable cold.

The central heating was turned off on the first of April, regardless of the weather. The huge boiler, which, antiquated, wasteful and marvellously powerful, kept the draughty house warm all through the winter, finished its task the moment March was over, and though for several years now, such had been the slowness of our northern spring, there had been protests, discussions, even decisions, nothing had ever been done, and the central heating still went off on April the first.

Nanny was even against fires after that date. There was no reason for this. She suffered from the cold as much as, if not more than, most people; but she had always been very mean with other people's property. Fires were lit, however, because Mrs. Lane insisted on it, but Nanny had various methods of sabotaging this course of action. Looks and sighs and mutterings went unnoticed, so she attacked the fuel supply. She would intercept Florence, the maid, a gentle shy girl from the village, and volunteer to carry the refilled coal scuttle into the drawing-room; then she would leave it outside. She would also seize any opportunity she had when left alone in that room to push the wood basket into a dark unaccustomed corner. When anybody complained of the lack of fuel, she would say briskly (or as briskly as she ever said anything): 'Well, do you really think it's cold enough? I hardly think it's really cold enough, you know.' And then occasionally the fire would be allowed to go out, and Nanny would be left with a sense of righteous victory.

This campaign took up most of her time for the few weeks after the central heating was turned off. They were probably the happiest weeks of her year, for in them she felt the mental stimulation which is the reward of the overworked.

Feliks came with them. It was his first visit to Harris: neither Anthony nor Judith had ever been much given to asking people there; and it was perhaps partly the feeling of achievement his having finally got there gave him which made him so extravagantly delighted with the place. He was eulogistic at meals, thereby immediately forfeiting the regard of Mrs. Lane, Sir Ralph and Nanny, who could none of them believe him to be sincere.

Judith knew that he was, and was glad after all that he had come. He had asked himself, unable, he said, to bear the humiliation of Baldwin's having been asked before he was; and Judith, quite unable to explain why Baldwin was coming at all, had half-heartedly agreed. As it was, though, he was an asset, for though Mrs. Lane was charming to Baldwin, it was an uneasy, over-laboured, charm, and Sir Ralph had retreated into age and silence.

Judith tried to talk to him, but could get nothing out of him. He had found a canvas bag in some old cupboard. It was a relic of the days when he had had, for a year or two, a passion for sailing, and had raced an eight-metre with startling success, but it seemed to have hardly been used.

'This is going to make things much easier for me, much easier,' he said. 'I shall be able to take all my things out to the turning-round-house.'

There was an old creaking summer-house in the garden where he liked to sit when it was warm enough. The trouble was that it very seldom was warm enough, and he spent a good deal of time packing his 'ditty-bag' with all his account books, his writing materials, his scarf, and anything else he thought might come in useful—glue, a dictionary, a compass—and taking it out into the garden, only to be told, or to decide for himself, that he was bound to catch a chill. He would come back again and unpack. Then a shaft of bright sunlight would come through the window, the sky would be briefly blue and the whole process would start again.

'You did understand about the money,' Judith said. 'That it all came back?'

'Yes, yes indeed,' said Sir Ralph. 'I think I've sorted that out all right. Took some doing, but I've got it clear now. Haven't had my this month's statement, though, of course—I daresay he's made a muddle of it.'

'You see it was all a mistake,' said Judith. 'About Baldwin, I mean.'

'I'm not going to take a dictionary today,' said Sir Ralph. 'What on earth do I want a dictionary for?'

'*The Times* crossword?'

'Oh,' said Sir Ralph. 'Oh yes. You may be right. The crossword. But this is a German dictionary.'

'You see he never meant that, at all—it was my fault really,' said Judith. 'I was so frightened—when I heard, I mean—it was really my idea to give him money. . . .'

'I will take it,' said Sir Ralph. 'I will take it. You never know, do you? And besides, I like dictionaries—always have liked them—even German ones. Never ought to be without a dictionary.'

'But you do understand?' said Judith.

'What's that?' said Sir Ralph.

'I want you to understand about the mistake about Baldwin Reeves and the money and Anthony,' said Judith. 'It's very important to me that you should.'

'Do you know what the Vicar's Christian name is?' said Sir Ralph.

'No,' said Judith.

'I was listening to what you were saying,' said Sir Ralph, apologetically. 'Only it reminded me that I didn't know the Vicar's Christian name. On account of Baldwin being such a funny name for a fellow. Really a very funny name.'

'D'you like him?' asked Judith.

'Wardle?' said Sir Ralph.

'No, Baldwin,' said Judith.

'Oh yes yes yes,' said Sir Ralph. 'Very much indeed. You like everybody when you get to my age. Except Nanny. What about this, eh? This string. . . .'

'I wanted to talk to you about Baldwin,' said Judith. 'I thought you might be able to help.'

'Ah, as to that,' said Sir Ralph. 'I think I will take this string. I might want to do some gardening. Yes, I know, I know. I'm an old man you know, Judith, we mustn't forget that. I'm really an old, old man.'

'Oh I didn't mean,' said Judith, 'to bother you.'

'You could never bother me, my dear,' said Sir Ralph, smiling at her. 'But don't you worry. There's a point, you know, when one must let oneself grow old, just as there's a point when one must let oneself die. It's difficult to know when they're reached—very difficult. I don't want to read out there, do I, as well? I've got my accounts. Still, I might as well take a book, just in case.'

'What about a rug?' asked Judith.

'A rug. Yes,' said Sir Ralph. 'Though it really looks quite warm out there. Still there's no harm in taking a rug. Don't you worry my dear. There's nobody I wish better than you, nobody at all. No, don't bother. I can carry it. Gets a bit heavy, though. D'you know I think I will leave that dictionary behind after all?'

Mrs. Lane said to Judith: 'How charming Anthony's friend is.' That was what she had made him in her own mind—Anthony's faithful friend, courageous witness to the heroism of his superior officer—and as such she talked to him endlessly of her son. He let her do it, hoping it might make her look less ill.

He was interested besides, in hearing anything about Anthony. This odd hard house had been where he had lived and Baldwin's feelings about him were refreshed by it; in fact, Mrs. Lane's memories being all coloured by her state of mind, he found the house a more rewarding source of information about Anthony than his mother was.

'Did Anthony like this house?' he asked Nanny.

'No,' said Nanny.

He had lived here though. He had walked into this cold room, thrown down a coat or a stick, lain in this chair, been a light-eyed boy in the nursery.

'He was a boy, like all boys,' said Nanny sourly, in answer to his queries. 'They're all the same, boys.'

'All?' said Baldwin.

'Well, he had a way with him, that's all,' Nanny admitted. 'He was up to all the tricks I will say. I never knew a child like him. Not but what he was like all boys. They're all the same, all boys.'

'You mean he didn't like washing?' Baldwin asked. 'That sort of thing?'

'He was a clean boy, that I will say,' said Nanny. 'Not a sissy but always looked nice. Lovely complexion he had, all through school and everything, I remember. But untidy! You'd have needed three of me to clear up after him. Did he ever take off his coat without throwing it on the floor? And books and paints and pencils and forever taking off the dogs' collars and losing them.'

'Oh dogs,' said Baldwin. 'Was Bertie one of them?'

'Retrievers he had,' said Nanny. 'He always had retrievers. It was she liked this kind. He had retrievers. And bones all over the house and never did he hang up a coat of his own.'

'But when he married,' said Baldwin. 'Then of course it must have been different.'

'Nothing could change him,' said Nanny, with satisfaction.

'No, I daresay nothing did,' said Baldwin. 'Did you go to their wedding?'

'I went to London for it,' she said. 'We all went to London

for it. There's many would have given a lot to be in her shoes, though she suited him, I will say she suited him well enough. And the nursery now, the nicest room in the house, he used to say.' This admission, rashly made to a stranger she did not wholly trust, seemed at once to strike her as having been a mistake, for she began to mumble in a vaguely qualifying way.

'I can see he broke a lot of hearts,' said Baldwin unkindly.

'Well, I must be getting along,' Nanny said. 'They're all the same, all boys. Well, I must be getting along.' She bustled out of the room, quite as if she had something to do.

Later Baldwin walked up into the nursery, and found that the wide windows and some pale sunshine in which the dust danced made it what might well have been the nicest room in the house.

There was an ink-stained desk in the corner at which Anthony had presumably sat. In the thin face the light brown eyes had scanned, bored, the unrewarding country from this window: the voice had been here, had insulted, probably, that doting old Nanny; all those familiar movements had been made in this room. 'Oh, Baldwin,' he might have said, turning as if he had been waiting for him, 'Oh, Baldwin,' and made some demand on him, with which he would have without question complied.

The room had the look very much of being uninhabited, which made Baldwin feel quite simply the desolation of being dead, no matter how many demands might have been made, and acceded to, how much love willingly or unwillingly claimed.

As he went out of the room he vaguely registered it as being the one in which he and Judith were least likely to be disturbed, should it come to that. He did not go into the question of whether or not the fact of its being the room most still reminiscent of Anthony had anything to do with the pleasantness of his picture of Judith's seduction there. It was all too complicated.

The next thing now, it seemed to him, encouraged by his success with Mrs. Lane, was to charm Sir Ralph.

At first he surveyed him cautiously but with confidence, a military expert inspecting a beleaguered garrison which could not hope to hold out much longer. It was simply a question of finding the weaknesses in the ancient walls, of executing the campaign with the most possible dash and bravado. But in some extraordinary way the citadel remained impregnable. Through lunch, tea, dinner, the garden, the cold summer house, the draughty library, the campaign was waged, and failed.

At dinner Baldwin had all his forces out. Hardly a name in public life for the last fifty years but was evoked to help his cause. ('You must have known So-and-so—he was a friend of mine.') Some or other variation of this method had usually worked in the past. There was nearly always a snobbery somewhere, of however rare a variety, through which an assault could be made. Here there was either none or one so vast as to imply: 'Of course you know all the right people—otherwise you wouldn't be in my house.' Baldwin could not make up his mind which was the case, but nor could he believe that this tried old method would not somehow prove applicable in the end. Like a general with too many victories to his credit, he had become inflexible.

Advice on gardening and estate management ('Gavin Miller was telling me the other day that at Longdon—I expect you know it—he's turning over more and more to timber. Soft woods, of course'), on the Stock Exchange, on tax evasion, on the desirability of litigation ('I hear you're having some difficulty with a tenant farmer'), all provoked the same polite, vague and increasingly irrelevant replies. The recent years of Sir Ralph's life had been quiet: his daughter-in-law's animosity was so much a habit for both of them that it had assumed a sort of propriety in his estimation, and by the few people outside his family whom he did see he was treated with deference but not taken seriously, not listened to much, but humoured, as a well-known eccentric, so that conversationally he had had things pretty well his own way. He found the battery to which he was now exposed—and by someone of, as far as he could remember, the most regrettable character—unusual and altogether unwelcome. He retreated a little further into the refuge of apparent feeble-mindedness.

'Didn't you once own an eight-metre, sir?'

'Ah, we can't all be spacemen, Mr. Baldwin.'

'No, indeed. I'm sure I should prefer the Solent to outer space. I spent a good deal of time last summer on a rather nice converted six-metre belonging to a friend of mine. He keeps her in the Hamble.'

'Nanny, I think Mr. Baldwin would like some bread. The Hamble, yes, how delightful.'

'His name is Mr. Reeves, Fa,' said Mrs. Lane.

'You kept her at Cowes, I suppose?' said Baldwin. 'No, I won't have any bread thank you.'

'No, no, Good Heavens no,' said Sir Ralph. 'We lived in London then. We never went to Cowes except for the sailing.'

'Oh,' said Baldwin. 'They're lovely boats, of course, aren't they? But awfully expensive to keep up. Paget, whom I met the other day, was telling me he doesn't think he'll be able to afford his much longer.'

'Nanny, did you give Mr. Baldwin some bread?' said Sir Ralph.

'No, I won't have any really, thank you so much,' said Baldwin.

'He doesn't want any,' said Nanny.

'Really?' said Sir Ralph, apparently surprised.

'No, really, thank you,' said Baldwin. 'Was he in the class when you had your boat—Paget, I mean?'

'We had a wretched vet here once,' said Sir Ralph with sudden animation. 'Absolutely without the most elementary knowledge of hygiene—a filthy fellow. If you had a sick animal you could be quite sure it would catch something far worse if he came to see it. He was covered in germs. I used to make him stand in a bucket of Lysol before I'd let him into the stables.'

'Oh did you?' said Baldwin.

'His name was Paget,' said Sir Ralph.

Afterwards Judith said to Baldwin, 'I think he likes to be left alone really.'

'Oh no, he's a splendid old thing,' said Baldwin. 'I enjoy talking to him. We shall get on very well.'

Judith had not imagined him thick-skinned. If she had not known whether or not she wanted him to succeed with Sir Ralph, she had certainly not known how much importance she would attach to the outcome of his effort. She had not expected to see him fail so dismally at his own game. She thought it a discreditable game, but that did not seem to alter the fact that she preferred to see him succeed at it.

Success in fact had come to be what he stood for in her mind, a man whose unscrupulous charm no one could resist. When it was successful the unscrupulousness could not discount the charm; indeed in Judith's eyes, she now began to realise, it had in an unreasonable sort of way rather added to it; but when, face to face with this frail defender of some other faith, Baldwin's confidence faltered and he began to bungle, Judith found herself shocked. She began to wonder what it was that had seemed so powerful about him.

Baldwin, however, had sniffed the breeze of victory. Mrs. Lane, with whom he had anticipated the greatest possible difficulty, had fallen without a fight. The old man, in spite of a certain foolish reluctance, was bound to succumb before long. And then new, and not uninteresting, vistas opened.

There was Harris, for instance. Married to Judith, he would probably be asked to take the place over, perhaps even before Sir Ralph's death. It would be a little difficult to manage, with Parliament, but they would be able to work something out. There would be some Lane money to help, and possibly Judith might have to spend a good deal of time up there while he was in London. The idea of being a country gentleman had never appealed to him before, but here in the north country there was a sort of rough practical feudalism among the Lane tenants which he had never come across before in his country house visiting, which tended to concentrate on the southern counties, and he began to see a sort of dignity in taking part in that way of life.

Any doubts he may have felt about Judith, about whether

he was rash to allow himself to feel so strongly about her, about how much Anthony was involved in what he felt for her, about whether she would ever trust him, were dissolved in this mood of optimism. Of course she was in love with him, of course she would be useful to him, of course he was going to be a tremendous success.

By lunch time on Sunday he had convinced himself that Sir Ralph was more or less won: it was simply that his manner was naturally surly.

Judith, feeling tired because she had stayed in bed so late that morning, was talking to Feliks who had been jealously reading the book reviews in the Sunday papers.

'I suppose Peter Flower's your Member here?' said Baldwin.

Judith looked up and would have spoken, but Sir Ralph said: 'Peter Flower, yes. Silly ass.'

Judith turned back to Feliks.

'A wonderfully safe seat, of course,' said Baldwin.

Sir Ralph said nothing.

'One hears rumours that he's going to retire, but he never seems quite to bring himself to the point,' said Baldwin.

'Retire?' said Sir Ralph. 'Yes, he's retiring. Sent the committee a letter the other day. Good riddance. That's what we all thought.'

'Really?' said Baldwin. 'It's not officially announced yet, is it?'

'No,' said Sir Ralph.

'Nice seat for somebody,' said Baldwin.

There was a pause.

'I wonder if they've got anyone in mind,' said Baldwin. 'A local man, I mean.'

'Aren't any local men,' said Sir Ralph.

Baldwin, encouraged by the fact that Sir Ralph seemed for once to be paying attention to the conversation, said cheerfully and as it were jokingly: 'There's me, of course.'

Feliks looked up. 'Surely you couldn't abandon your faithful following in wherever it is?' he said.

'I could,' said Baldwin. 'I'm due for a safer seat anyway.

There's not much hope of winning that one back now.'

'I can't quite see you in the part of the country Member,' said Feliks.

'D'you know, I was only thinking this morning how much it would become me?' said Baldwin. 'I like this country. One feels one can breathe up here.'

'What a good idea,' said Mrs. Lane, quite suddenly, from the end of the table. 'Don't you think so, Fa?'

'Excellent, my dear, excellent,' said Sir Ralph.

Baldwin, surprised but delighted at the way things were going, began to take it all the more seriously.

'Of course the rest of the committee would have to know who I was,' he said. 'I'm on the Central Office list, but then I think these far-flung constituencies are often predisposed against a Central Office recommendation before they've even seen him.'

'Yes,' said Mrs. Lane. 'Suggest Mr. Reeves to Elliot, Fa.'

'He is a neighbour of ours,' said Sir Ralph to Baldwin. 'A charming fellow. He goes in for pheasant farming. He's just started it.'

'I thought you disliked him, Fa,' said Mrs. Lane. 'But if you're on good terms with him now all the better. It makes it easier for you to suggest Mr. Reeves to him as a suitable candidate.'

'Candidate?' said Sir Ralph. 'Do you wish to take up pheasant farming, Mr. Baldwin?'

'No, not exactly,' said Baldwin, thinking it might be wiser to change the subject for the moment. 'It must be very interesting though. Does he do it on a large scale?'

'A very large scale,' said Sir Ralph.

'Mr. Reeves wants to stand for Parliament, Fa,' said Mrs. Lane, persisting. 'Why don't you suggest to Elliot that he should succeed Peter Flower?'

'Oh, he's thought of that,' said Sir Ralph. 'He'd make a complete ass of himself.'

'Not Elliot,' said Mrs. Lane. 'Mr. Reeves.'

Sir Ralph said gently, 'Mr. Reeves knows why I am unable to recommend him to any position of trust.'

Judith, who had been waiting for this, had not guessed that it would be administered so directly. After a moment of admiration for the old man, she found her eyes full of tears. She had not realised until that moment how much she had wanted a husband.

Nanny, seeing her tears, brightened, and looked round the table optimistically. Perhaps something was going to happen.

Mrs. Lane turned pale. However vague her suspicions, they were there, and she knew that they threatened her life. She put a hand up to her hair and said vaguely: 'If Anthony—if only Anthony could have had the seat. . . .'

Baldwin thought, 'I could have sworn he'd forgotten all about the money.' Catching sight of Judith's tears, he thought, 'She's crying for me. That's good. I'll take her away from here.' He felt full of tenderness for her.

Feliks, feeling out of it, thought resentfully that he might have enjoyed the week-end more if the train fare had been less.

After lunch Baldwin, feeling now that to have lost the Lanes was nothing if he had gained Judith, led her firmly off to the old nursery and said, 'Now we can talk.'

'What about?' said Judith.

'What would you like to talk about?' he said.

'Oh nothing, nothing,' she said.

'Thomas Hood is more fortunate than I,' said Baldwin.

'Oh, Thomas,' she said.

'Can you dismiss him so?' asked Baldwin.

'I used Thomas as an escape from you,' said Judith. 'You know that and you know how pleased you were because you felt that through Thomas my fall had been accomplished, I had been brought low, I could no longer fool myself I was any better than you. I know I treated Thomas badly, but it seems to me that is a chance we all take all the time. Anthony distressed you, you me, I Thomas. But Anthony's is the only victory because he is dead. For us the process goes on, and for the moment is reversed because we are neither of us as wicked as we should like to be. Thomas is making me feel guilty, I shall make you unhappy because in the course of engineering a seduction which was to be the conquest not only of me but of Anthony you have fallen slightly in love. Also of course the seduction has failed.'

'I see I have a lot to learn from you,' said Baldwin. 'You make my attempts at ruthlessness seem naïve.'

'I am only being reasonable,' said Judith.

'What a destructive quality reason seems to be,' said Baldwin. 'Has it failed, the seduction?'

'As you say, reason is destructive,' said Judith.

'You know, I quite thought you—how shall I say it?—reciprocated my feelings,' said Baldwin.

'I did. I do.'

'But you resist them?'

'What we feel for each other is really a passion for power,' said Judith. 'We want to destroy each other by making the other fall in love with us—we challenge each other, that's all. You want to revenge on me the fact that you loved Anthony, I on you the fact that I sometimes hated him. But reason, as you say, has destroyed it all.'

She faced him with a sort of subdued excitement which he could not quite understand. Finally he said: 'I believe I once congratulated you, do you remember, for combining so much passion with so much stability. But now I see they are more closely connected than I thought, and the passion was for the stability—is it possible to be passionately stable? I suppose you would think me hysterical if I asked you whether you had a heart?'

'A heart?'

'Whether you love anything.'

'I suppose discipline is a part of love?' she asked. 'It's a long time since I had to put love into practice, so I find it hard to remember. All the same, there are things I love. Perhaps you are right in thinking one of them is stability—or could you call it God?'

'No, I don't think you could,' said Baldwin. 'But you are quite up to date. Isn't God rather the thing these days?'

'I believe He is among the very young, but I don't know

much about that. Thomas talks about it sometimes.'

'I told Thomas I was going to marry you,' said Baldwin.

'Why?'

'I thought I was. Also it gave me pleasure. I was jealous, you see.'

'Poor Thomas.'

'But you can tell him it's not so.'

'No.'

'No?'

'No, I shan't tell him—not yet at any rate. It would be better to leave it.'

'You don't need him now you are disposing of me,' said Baldwin.

'I was thinking of him. But perhaps there is something in that.'

'And I'm to accept defeat so humbly?'

'What else is there for you to do?'

'Nothing,' said Baldwin. After a pause he said, 'Is this all because I was snubbed by your husband's grandfather?'

But that was something which, for once, she did not feel capable of going into.

'I suppose he may have had a little to do with it,' she said. 'And Anthony, too.'

'Oh, I can't compete with Anthony,' he said.

It had begun to rain. They stood at separate windows, looking out on to the wide moors.

'I miss him, all the same,' said Baldwin.

12

After the panel game, Baldwin usually got a little drunk on beer. He liked neither beer nor being drunk, but it was what he seemed to need in that particular situation. The long slow intake and the resulting blur—he found no exhilaration in beer-drinking—the dreariness of the particular pub in which he chose to drink, the failure of its inmates to arouse in him the faintest flicker of interest, soothed him, and provided the soporific he needed after the intense and irritable liveliness of mind brought on by the exercise of his wits. He exercised them to good effect, and could be called, as far as television was concerned, a success. Already he was in the process of arranging to appear regularly in a discussion programme, with the aim of furthering what he regarded as his serious career, the political one.

All this led to his greeting more amiably than usual an unimportant advertising agent called Charlesworth whom he met in Victoria one evening. The man offered him a drink and Baldwin accepted, because though he had already had his post panel game fill of beer, he was in no particular hurry to go back to his flat. Also he felt like talking, and Charlesworth, being, he considered, of no account, was the sort of person with whom he found it easiest to talk freely. They went into a pub.

'How do the constituents like their candidate's television fame?' asked the advertising agent, with rather sycophantic jollity. 'Going down well, I daresay?'

'With some, with some,' said Baldwin, looking round with unshaken contentment. 'With some.' He smiled benignly. 'And how's the advertising world? Not that I want you to tell me.'

'Oh, not so bad,' said Charlesworth. 'My trouble is. . . .'

'No, no, I said don't tell me,' said Baldwin. 'Advertising is a perfectly revolting profession.'

'I don't know that I'd go as far as that,' said Charlesworth, a little uneasily.

'Yes it is, it's revolting,' said Baldwin, happily. 'Take politics, take industry—take journalism, like my friend Herman here. . . .'

'Harman,' said Harman. He had been sitting at the bar not far away and had come up to join them.

'You're always in pubs, Harman,' said Baldwin.

'I know,' said Harman.

'You strike me as a lonely fellow,' said Baldwin, pleasantly. 'I don't believe you have any friends.'

'I haven't,' said Harman.

'How very admirable,' said Baldwin, whose sleepiness was beginning to give way to a sort of serene enthusiasm.

'What about that story?' asked Harman. 'The one you were going to write and I was going to take you to see Blow about?'

'I gave up the idea,' said Baldwin. 'I got sidetracked somehow.'

'You know they're making a film of the Lane incident, don't you?' said Harman. 'Are you in on that?'

'No,' said Baldwin.

'Not?' said Harman. 'I should have thought you'd be getting a fat fee as an adviser or something of the sort. They must be crazy not to have got hold of you. Why don't you do something about it?'

'They approached me,' said Baldwin. 'But I was unable to accept their offer.'

'Oh,' said Harman, thinking quickly. 'You mean because you're expecting an election this year?'

Baldwin laughed loudly and clapped him on the back. 'You old newshound,' he said.

Harman, who was a small man, winced and spilt some of his beer.

'What do you think I'm paid for?' he said irritably. 'There must be a good reason for you to pass up the money and prestige you could make out of that affair now. But don't worry. Don't tell me. I'll read it in the newspapers, I don't doubt.'

'I could, I suppose, have made some honest money out of it,' said Baldwin. 'How odd. Or fairly honest. But one must live in the future, not the past, don't you agree? And I don't feel that I am destined to make my mark in films.'

Harman shrugged, unappeased.

Baldwin began euphoristically to think of the fields in which he was destined to make his mark, surveying the smoky saloon as a drunken emperor might benignly watch the soldiers he was tomorrow to lead to further glories carousing after a victorious battle.

'Have the other half,' said Harman.

'How simple life is,' said Baldwin, pushing over his glass.

'When one has faced the fact of one's solitude. For the true solitary ambition has no limits. I feel splendid. What would you most like to see me do?'

'God knows,' said Harman, disapprovingly. 'I leave it to you.'

For a moment Baldwin paused, suddenly gazing through the mists of his intoxication into a not unfamiliar abyss where loneliness and failure monstrously loomed; then looking solemnly at Harman he said with resolution: 'Yes, leave it to me. I'll think of something.'

'Of course you will,' said Charlesworth, suddenly and heartily. He had been eyeing a blonde on the other side of the room and paying no attention to the conversation, but now beerily remembered that Baldwin was a useful man to keep in with.

'Oh shut up,' said Baldwin.

Fisher and Miss Vanderbank were having an early lunch. They had taken sandwiches into Green Park, and Bertie had gone with them for the exercise. He scampered from group to group (it was sunny and the park was full) licking the faces of lovers and stealing the sandwiches of typists, taking the bread from the mouths of pigeons and a bar of chocolate gently but firmly from the hand of a justly enraged child. Miss Vanderbank shrieked prettily, but he ignored her. Fisher, embarrassed, had to pursue him.

'I wonder if it won't be me you finally marry,' said Hanescu.

'I don't think so, do you?' said Judith.

'You ought not to remain childless—that horrible Nanny made me think of it. Motherhood would suit you. And then of course I like the idea of founding a dynasty, like all self-made men.'

'I'm a great rejecter of experience, you know,' said Judith. 'Perhaps I'm wrong.'

'The experience of Baldwin might have done you good, though not as much as it would have done him,' said Feliks.

'But then I don't think you need experience. I think you knew it all when you were born. We won't have Nanny in the house, of course. How angry the Lanes would be if we married. I'm afraid there's a certain strata of society in which I shall never be accepted—not the highest of all, I'm all right there, but the next. Ah well, we mustn't be morbid about the Lanes, either of us.'

'No,' said Judith.

'And you could do a series on bringing up children,' said Feliks. 'And I daresay we could fix you up with one of the better Sunday papers. Child guidance, that's the sort of thing.'

'Miss Vanderbank would hate it,' said Judith.

'We could fix her up with Fisher,' said Feliks. 'A double ceremony. It would be an excuse for redecorating the office.'

'I don't know about that particular excuse,' said Judith. 'But I'm sure you'll find another. In which case I insist on abolishing those rosebuds.'

'You're quite right,' said Feliks. 'I've gone off wallpaper anyway. We'll have paint in wonderful colours. Let's plan it. Have you got a piece of paper? I need a new desk. Substances—we must have more substances. Pink for Fisher?'

Judith smiled, comfortably assuming a familiar role.

'Certainly not,' she said. 'Anyway, the whole thing sounds far too expensive.'

RECENT AND FORTHCOMING TITLES FROM VALANCOURT BOOKS

Michael Arlen	Hell! said the Duchess
Frank Baker	The Birds
H. E. Bates	Fair Stood the Wind for France
Walter Baxter	Look Down in Mercy
Charles Beaumont	The Hunger and Other Stories
David Benedictus	The Fourth of June
Paul Binding	Harmonica's Bridegroom
John Blackburn	A Scent of New-Mown Hay
Thomas Blackburn	A Clip of Steel
John Braine	Room at the Top
	The Vodi
	Life at the Top
Michael Campbell	Lord Dismiss Us
Hunter Davies	Body Charge
Jennifer Dawson	The Ha-Ha
A. E. Ellis	The Rack
Barry England	Figures in a Landscape
Michael Frayn	The Tin Men
	The Russian Interpreter
	Towards the End of the Morning
	A Very Private Life
	Sweet Dreams
Gillian Freeman	The Liberty Man
	The Leather Boys
	The Leader
Rodney Garland	The Heart in Exile
Stephen Gilbert	The Landslide
	Monkeyface
	The Burnaby Experiments
	Ratman's Notebooks
Martyn Goff	The Plaster Fabric
	The Youngest Director
Stephen Gregory	The Cormorant
Alex Hamilton	Beam of Malice
Thomas Hinde	The Day the Call Came
Claude Houghton	I Am Jonathan Scrivener
	This Was Ivor Trent
Fred Hoyle	The Black Cloud
Alan Judd	The Devil's Own Work

James Kennaway	The Mind Benders
	The Cost of Living Like This
Cyril Kersh	The Aggravations of Minnie Ashe
Gerald Kersh	Fowlers End
	Nightshade and Damnations
Francis King	To the Dark Tower
	Never Again
	The Dark Glasses
	The Man on the Rock
C.H.B. Kitchin	Ten Pollitt Place
	The Book of Life
	A Short Walk in Williams Park
Hilda Lewis	The Witch and the Priest
John Lodwick	Brother Death
Robin Maugham	Behind the Mirror
Michael Nelson	A Room in Chelsea Square
Beverley Nichols	Crazy Pavements
Oliver Onions	The Hand of Kornelius Voyt
J.B. Priestley	Benighted
	The Magicians
	Saturn Over the Water
	The Thirty-First of June
	Salt is Leaving
Piers Paul Read	Monk Dawson
Forrest Reid	Brian Westby
	The Tom Barber Trilogy
	Denis Bracknel
Nevil Shute	Landfall
	An Old Captivity
Andrew Sinclair	The Raker
	Gog
	The Facts in the Case of E. A. Poe
David Storey	Radcliffe
	Pasmore
	Saville
John Wain	Hurry on Down
	The Smaller Sky
	A Winter in the Hills
Hugh Walpole	The Killer and the Slain
Keith Waterhouse	There is a Happy Land
	Billy Liar
Colin Wilson	Ritual in the Dark
	The Philosopher's Stone

CPSIA information can be obtained
at www.ICGtesting.com
Printed in the USA
LVOW12s0332240118
563806LV00001B/16/P